First published in Great Britain 2018
by Egmont UK Limited, The Yellow Building,
1 Nicholas Road, London W11 4AN

© 2018 Universal Studios. Jurassic World: Fallen Kingdom
is a trademark and copyright of Universal Studios and
Amblin Entertainment, Inc. All Rights Reserved.

ISBN 978 1 4052 9163 7
68662/001

Printed in UK

A Junior Novel

A novelization by David Lewman

Based on the screenplay written by
Derek Connolly & Colin Trevorrow and
characters created by Michael Crichton.

CHAPTER 1

We altered the course of natural history.
This is a necessary correction.
—Dr. Ian Malcolm

Just off the coast of Isla Nublar, a small submarine cut through the dark ocean waters, heading toward the abandoned Jurassic World lagoon. The dinosaur theme park had been closed for years and was in a state of sad disrepair. The two men operating the sub had orders to retrieve an important sunken object.

Above the surface of the water, no stars shone in the night sky. Rain poured down.

Inside a guard station at the surface next to the lagoon, a technician worked the controls that opened the lagoon's algae-covered steel gates and spoke into a mic. "Where are you, Marine One?"

"We've just passed the gates," the sub's pilot answered.

"Roger that," the technician said. "Air One, clear for takeoff. Begin tracking."

Behind him, a helicopter lifted off into the sky. "Copy that," said its pilot. "Tracking on." As the technician watched, the helicopter flew over the lagoon, tracking the sub.

Inside the cramped quarters of the sub, the two men were sweating. "Relax," the pilot said to the man beside him. "Anything here'd be dead by now."

The sub's bright floodlights lit up bleached white bones on the bottom of the lagoon. "There she is," the pilot said. "The Indominus Rex."

He steered the submarine right over the dinosaur skeleton. The other man operated the sub's robotic arms, grabbing a rib bone and sawing it off.

"Air One, specimen collected," the pilot radioed. "Sending to the surface."

"Copy that," the helicopter pilot radioed back.

As the men in the sub sent the bone up in a sealed glass tube attached to an inflatable balloon with a flashing red beacon, a huge and ominous shadow passed silently behind the submarine and her unsuspecting crew.

The rib bone broke through the surface of the water and bobbed in the rough waves. The men in the helicopter spotted the beacon, opened the copter's door, and snagged the bone using a mechanical claw lowered from a long cable. "Land One," the helicopter pilot radioed to the technician in the guard station, "we've got what we came for. We're coming back for you."

"Roger that," the technician said. "Marine One, I need to close the lagoon gates. Clear out of there."

"Understood," the submarine pilot said. "We're heading out. Stand by."

But at that moment, a massive silhouette appeared in the water. The man who'd worked the robot arms peered through the submarine's cockpit window. Suddenly, he saw a gigantic eye!

In the helicopter, the submarine's signal flickered out on the instrument panel. The pilot looked puzzled. "Marine One, confirm your position. We lost your signal."

But there was no answer.

The helicopter landed near the guard station. Then . . .

BOOOOM! The ground shook. Leaves fell from the trees. "What was that?" the pilot asked, alarmed.

In the guard station, the technician spoke into his headset, starting to sound a little frantic. "Marine One, I've gotta close the lagoon gates. Confirm you're out." Silence. "Can you hear me, Marine One? Confirm your position!"

In the helicopter, the crew members spotted what had caused the loud boom. They frantically waved their arms, trying to get the attention of the technician. But he couldn't hear them over the sound of the helicopter. Finally, he noticed that they were pointing behind him.

He turned around just as lightning flashed, illuminating a massive *Tyrannosaurus rex* looming high above him, her colossal head and razor-sharp teeth just feet away! *ROOOAAAWWRRR!*

Terrified, the technician ran toward the helicopter, but it was already taking off. "Throw him the ladder!" shouted one of the guys in the copter. A rope ladder unrolled from the helicopter. The technician grabbed it and climbed as the helicopter rose.

CHOMP! The *T. rex* bit the rope ladder below the technician! The rope went taut. It was a tug-of-war between the *T. rex* and the helicopter, with the technician caught in between.

"Cut it!" yelled a crew member. "Let him go!"

Other crew members started unhooking the ladder. "No, wait!" screamed the technician.

SNAP! The rope ladder broke where the *T. rex* had grabbed it with her teeth. The technician held on, dangling from the upper half of the ladder as the helicopter started to fly away.

The technician breathed a sigh of relief. That had been close, but now he was safe—

WHOOOSH! A *Mosasaurus*, one of the largest reptiles to ever hunt the seas, roared up out of the lagoon with its gigantic mouth wide open! *CHOMP!* The *Mosasaurus* engulfed the screaming technician!

The chopper flew safely into the night sky. Its crew members stared as the *Mosasaurus* crashed back down into the water.

With the Indominus Rex bone locked in a high-tech metal container, the helicopter flew away over the mountains. The *Mosasaurus* leapt out of the water and plunged back into the inky depths. *SPLASH!!!* Then she whipped her huge tail and swam through the lagoon's open gates into the ocean.

She was free.

CHAPTER
2

Of course I think that we should allow our
beautiful dinos to be taken out by the volcano.
—Dr. Ian Malcolm

Three years later . . .

A television news report showed a smoking volcano.
An anchorwoman's voice said, "Isla Nublar, the former
site of the ill-fated theme park Jurassic World, now
faces a new threat. Its volcano, long thought to be
dormant, has recently become active. Geologists
predict an extinction-level event will soon kill off the
last dinosaurs known to exist on the planet. And that
has raised a serious debate on the floor of the Senate
today. Should the United States government step in

and rescue these creatures, or should we allow the dinosaurs to once again become extinct?"

The picture on the TV switched from the volcano to a man leaving a government building. Ducking reporters' questions, he covered his face with his hands. "Former Jurassic World scientist Dr. Henry Wu, stripped of all credentials after being found guilty of bioethical misconduct, refused to comment," reported the anchorwoman.

The TV was on in the office of the Dinosaur Protection Group, but the volunteers there were too busy to watch it. They talked on the phone, tapped away at computers, and painted protest posters with sayings like "Save the Dinos" and "They were here first!"

A soft chime from across the expansive room signaled the arrival of the elevator. The old, prewar doors began to open, but then stopped halfway. Inside the elevator was Claire Dearing, who precariously balanced a tray of coffees in one hand and shoved the elevator doors open with the other.

Claire crossed the room and deposited a cup of coffee on the desk of Zia Rodriguez, a tattooed Paleoveterinarian in her late twenties who spoke into her headset, trying to raise support for the Dinosa

Protection Group's efforts. Since patience wasn't her strong suit, Zia wasn't the world's greatest fund raiser, and her latest potential donor was slipping through her fingers.

"Yes," she said with an exhausted sigh, "but your vocal support would send Congress a clear message that dinosaurs are living creatures with real emotions who don't deserve to be abandoned."

Claire put down the tray of coffees. She knew that Zia's talents were in caring for dinosaurs and not talking on phones, so she motioned for Zia to hand over the receiver, and once she did, Claire was immediately in her element.

"Hi, Congresswoman Delgado. My name is Claire. I'm the lead organizer here," said Claire as she moved around the room seeing to other matters while talking on the phone at the same time. She was a multitasking maven, applying corporate management skills for good.

"Our mission at the Dinosaur Protection Group is to secure funds for a safe, natural habitat for these creatures," said Claire, before stopping abruptly and _____ to what was being said on the other end of

She took a deep breath. "Yes. I am the same Claire Dearing who was the operations manager at Jurassic World. And yes, I do feel responsible for what happened there. That's why I'm here doing what I'm doing now."

Continuing, Claire stole away to a private corner of the office. "Do you have kids, Congresswoman? Well, your kids—an entire generation—have grown up in a world where dinosaurs exist. And now they'll have to watch them go extinct. Again. Unless people like you make a difference. Literally you. Right here. Right now."

Claire waited for the Congresswoman to answer. When she did, Claire breathed a sigh of relief and said, "Thank you," before hanging up the phone and moving back to handing out coffees.

She eventually found herself at Franklin Webb's desk. Franklin barely looked at Claire when she set down a cup of coffee. The focused twenty-four-year-old was much more comfortable with computers than people.

Claire took a look at his screen and saw a video of herself giving a talk to a class of children. "How many views do we have?" she asked.

"Two or three," Franklin said.

"Million?" asked Claire, surprised.

"Ha! No. Two or three hundred," answered Franklin, leaving Claire to deflate like a balloon while he continued. "The kids are cute, but the video's boring. The attention span on the internet is seventeen seconds. You have to do something more than just make a good argument."

Claire thought on this. "Okay, how do we get their attention?"

"I don't know." Franklin shrugged. "Put a guy in a *T. rex* suit on a motorcycle or something." Claire gave him a doubtful look. "They don't teach viral marketing at MIT," he said. "I'm doing my best here."

Claire looked around the room at all the idealistic young people depending on her. "We're running out of time," she said.

"It's on," Zia said, referring to the TV.

On the screen a man in a suit was speaking outside a government building: "The committee will not recommend any legislative actions regarding the de-extinct creatures on Isla Nublar. This is an act of God, and while . . ."

Claire stopped paying attention to the TV and allowed the man's voice to trail off. She knew what this meant, and said as much to her team of volunteers, "They're all going to die . . . and no one cares."

"*We* do," Franklin insisted.

As Claire smiled at Zia and Franklin, her cell phone buzzed. She answered it. "Hello? Yes, this is Claire Dearing." Suddenly, her expression changed. Her look and her voice became excited. "Yes, I'll hold!

CHAPTER 3

With all due respect, Senator—the almighty
is not part of this equation. . . .
—Dr. Ian Malcolm

Along the northern coast of California, waves crashed on a rocky shore. A black car made its way up the coastal highway, heading for a massive stone mansion set in a forest of redwood trees. The mansion was called Lockwood Estate after its owner, who had invited Claire to come see him. She'd left the office immediately.

Claire peered out the window of the limousine, looking up at the towering gates. She was full of hope that Sir Benjamin Lockwood would help the Dinosaur Protection Group save the dinosaurs.

Once inside the mansion, Claire waited in a reception hall to be led in to see Sir Lockwood. Scanning the painted portraits hanging on the walls, she recognized John Hammond. As she leaned in for a closer look, a voice behind her said, "John Hammond, the father of Jurassic Park."

Claire turned to see a man in a dapper dark suit smiling at her. "Hello, Claire. I'm Eli Mills." They shook hands. "I work for Mr. Lockwood, running his foundation. Your park, Jurassic World, was Mr. Lockwood's favorite place. Better than he and Hammond ever imagined."

"They must have been quite the team," Claire said.

Speaking in a Scottish accent, Mills said, "'A dreamer and a philanthropist, limited only by imagination.' That's my John Hammond imitation. It's terrible."

Claire laughed. She liked Mills.

"Please follow me into the library," Mills said, gesturing.

The library rose two stories to a curved glass roof. Tall wooden bookshelves were stuffed with books.

The walls on the far side of the room were actually floor-to-ceiling glass cases that held elaborate dioramas of dinosaurs fighting, feeding, and caring for their young. Dinosaur skeletons were mounted on display, including a massive *Triceratops horridus* skull in the middle of the room.

"This house is where it all began, you know," Mills said. "Jurassic Park, all of it. They built a custom lab in the sub-basement. Extracted the first DNA from amber right beneath our feet. Well, that's the past. But *this* is the future."

Mills gestured toward an elaborate model of a mountainous jungle by the sea. Plastic dinosaurs were walking down a ramp from a ship, two by two. Other dinosaurs stomped across the rolling green hills.

"We have a piece of land," Mills explained. "A *sanctuary*. Protected by natural barriers and fully self-sustaining. Our environmentalists say the climate will support all the species currently on Isla Nublar."

Claire could hardly believe it. "A sanctuary! You're going to save them!"

"No, Ms. Dearing," said a voice, "*we* are going to save them."

She turned to see Sir Benjamin Lockwood, a man

in his eighties, entering the library in a wheelchair. Claire could sense, from his slumped posture in the chair, that he was not in good health. He rolled right up to the model of the dinosaur sanctuary. "This was John Hammond's dream, you know. Letting them live in peace. No fences, no cages, no tourists. As Mother Earth intended."

"Thank you," Claire said, gesturing toward the model. "It's wonderful."

"It's the right thing to do," Lockwood said firmly.

Up on the second level of the library, she spotted a young girl peeking down. Claire smiled at her, but the girl ducked away.

A nurse appeared in an open door and gently called, "Sir Lockwood."

Lockwood nodded, saying, "Time for my medicine. Excuse me. We *will* save them, Claire. We *have* to. Thank you for coming. Eli will fill you in on the details." He rolled out of the room.

"Does he have children?" Claire asked Mills, thinking of the girl she'd seen up on the second level.

"A grandchild, Maisie," Mills answered. "His daughter and her husband died in a car accident. Come, we'll talk in my office."

Mills's office was full of communications equipment and filing cabinets. Claire and Eli studied a detailed map of Isla Nublar. The volcano was clearly marked on the north end of the island.

"So," she asked, "what do you need from me?"

"There was a tracking system in place at Jurassic World," Mills explained. "Radio frequency identification chips in each dinosaur."

Claire nodded. "Yes, I remember." She didn't much like being reminded of the events during her last disastrous days at Jurassic World. Like the Indominus Rex clawing out its identification chip and then going on a rampage.

"So if we could access that tracking system," Mills continued, "our ability to locate and capture the animals would increase tenfold. We could—"

"Save lives," Claire said, her thoughts returning to the present.

"Exactly," Mills said, smiling. "We need your handprint to access the bunker where the tracking system was headquartered."

"And to activate the tracking system," Claire said, holding up her palm. "My handprint is yours."

Mills looked her in the eye. "But what I really

need is *you*. No one knows the park as well as you do. We need that expertise."

"How many species are you trying to extract?"

Mills flipped through images of dinosaurs on his computer. "Eleven for sure. More if we can. Time's against us, I'm afraid." He paused on a *Velociraptor*. From Claire's reaction, Mills could tell she recognized the individual dinosaur. "That one in particular poses a real challenge for us."

"Blue," Claire said, remembering the only *Velociraptor* to survive the attack of the Indominus Rex.

Mills raised an eyebrow. "Potentially the second most intelligent piece of life on this planet. And the last of her kind. She must be preserved."

Claire shook her head. "She can pick up your scent a mile off. You'll never catch her."

"Well," Mills said, smiling, "we thought you might know someone who could help."

Claire knew exactly whom he meant. "Owen Grady won't help you."

Mills looked her straight in the eye. "Maybe you could convince him."

Owen Grady had spent several years training *Velociraptors* on Jurassic World. He had been on the island when things went terribly wrong. He and Claire had worked together then to survive, but most of the time, they did not see eye to eye.

Reluctantly Claire went to visit Owen high in the Sierra Nevada Mountains, where he was building a cabin for himself next to a lake, miles away from the nearest town. By the time Claire got there, Owen already knew why she'd come.

"Lockwood's little flunky called last week," he said, putting down his hammer. "Rescue operation. Save the dinosaurs from the island that's about to explode. What could possibly go wrong? It's insane. You can't do it."

"I have to try," Claire insisted. "When these animals are gone, that's it! There's no more."

Owen shook his head and offered her a bottle of water. "You can't make this better, Claire. You have to live with it."

Taking the water bottle, Claire decided to play her trump card.

"Blue's alive," she said. "You going to let her die?"

Owen was silent for a long moment. Then he said, "Yeah."

"You don't mean that!" Claire snapped. "You spent years of your life working with her. Come on, you *raised* her!"

Owen said nothing. He just picked up his hammer and resumed building.

"Why did I think you would care?" Claire said, getting back into her rental car. "Sorry to have wasted your valuable time."

She slammed the door and drove off. Owen watched her go. Then he turned back to his work.

That evening, just after sunset, Owen sat alone in his Airstream trailer in front of an old laptop, face aglow from flickering video images of times past. On his screen Owen watched a video from several years ago of him training Baby Blue and the other three Raptors: Echo, Delta, and Charlie, who were sadly lost to the Indominus Rex.

The Owen on the video clip said to the Raptors, "Take it easy. There's plenty of food," and put his hand up; and the four animals came to a halt like a unit, squad, or even a family.

Owen continued to watch the video as the dim lights painted his face inside the trailer. He smiled to

19

himself for a moment, remembering even after all this time how it felt to be with these animals, and realized that he had no choice.

If Blue was in danger, Owen had to save her.

CHAPTER
4

We resurrect the most lethal predators that
this planet has ever seen and then we're shocked to find
out they consider us prey?
—Dr. Ian Malcolm

At a small airport in Novato, California, Zia and Franklin handed their bags to a crew member, who stored them in the private plane supplied by Lockwood.

Franklin looked at the small plane nervously.

"Relax," Zia told him. "You're more likely to die riding a horse than in a plane."

"No, I'm not," Franklin disagreed. "Because I won't get on a horse. So my chances of dying on one are zero."

The pilot approached Claire, who was anxiously staring at the gate to the runway. "We're ready, ma'am," he said. "Let's get your expedition team on board."

Claire looked at her team of two young adults with little to no field experience and shuddered to think of the task that lay ahead. But somehow she managed to hide her concern and speak enthusiastically. "Okay, guys! Let's go!" As they boarded the plane, she took one more look back at the gate, hoping Owen would come running through it at the last possible second. He'd said no, but she still hoped he might change his mind. They could really use his expertise on this expedition.

He wasn't there.

But once Claire got inside the plane, she was surprised to see Owen already sprawled in a seat with a ratty baseball cap over his eyes. "You're here," she said, stunned.

Owen tipped up his cap and gave her a look that seemed to say, "What'd you expect?"

Claire introduced Owen to Zia and Franklin. Zia just nodded and calmly headed to the back of the plane. Franklin sat down next to Owen without shaking his hand or saying anything. He was too nervous to speak.

"Terrified of flying, huh?" Owen said.

"Would you ever ride a thousand-pound horse that's been abused its whole life?" Franklin asked. "Because that's the kind of risk we're taking here."

Owen shrugged. "I rode a motorcycle through the jungle with a pack of Raptors."

Franklin just stared at him for a moment. "We are not compatible."

The plane took off. Franklin gripped the armrest tightly.

As the plane reached Isla Nublar, Claire and Owen gazed through the windows down at the abandoned island. Smoke rose from the volcano. They could see the old Aviary where the *Pteranodons* once lived. It was now so covered in vines it was barely recognizable. They caught each other's eyes, remembering the carnage they'd seen on this island.

The plane passed over the Jurassic World gates, cracked and covered in jungle growth, and landed on a small dirt runway. A powerful, heavily armed man was waiting, standing in front of three similarly armed trappers and containment workers.

He approached the plane as Claire walked out onto the steps, and before she could get a word out, the man introduced himself: "Ken Wheatley. Welcome back to Jurassic World."

Claire looked past Wheatley to a makeshift base camp. There were several heavily armored vehicles, guarded by men with tranquilizer rifles. "This is some operation," she said.

"Mr. Lockwood takes his humanitarian efforts seriously," Wheatley said with a tight grin. "Woe to the unprepared."

Zia and Franklin climbed down from the plane. Wheatley spoke to Zia first. "The Paleoveterinarian. You go to some kinda school for that?"

Annoyed by this question, Zia just said, "I did," in a flat voice.

Wheatley turned to Franklin. "And you're the computer guy?"

"Systems architect," Franklin corrected him. "'Computer guy' kinda makes it sound like I work at a store where they also sell refrigerators."

But Wheatley had already moved on. "And which

one is the Raptor wrangler?"

Owen stepped off the plane wearing a hoodie and plastic sunglasses. "Animal behaviorist," he said, taking an instant dislike to Wheatley. He noticed Wheatley's pistol and rifle. "And you're, what, the Great White Hunter?"

Now it was Wheatley's turn to make a correction. "Expedition facilitator," he said, his smile coldly sarcastic. He didn't like Owen, either. "This way," he grunted, leading them toward the base-camp tents.

"Man, it's hot here," Franklin said, picking up his bag.

"It's about to get a whole lot hotter," Zia said, looking off at the volcano spewing smoke and fire.

Owen looked at the volcano with concern. "Hammond didn't think the volcano would be a problem when he built this place?"

"It's been dormant for a thousand years," Claire explained. "Experts swore it was extinct."

"Experts," Wheatley sneered with contempt.

At this, Claire shared a look with Owen. There was something about this guy that made them both uneasy. But with the enormous task at hand, they pushed this feeling aside and continued on.

"How much time do we have before she blows up?"

Owen asked, nodding toward the volcano.

"Our volcanologist says it could happen anytime now," Wheatley said. "The tremors are getting more frequent."

"Anytime now? Boy, that's comforting," said Franklin nervously. "I mean, aren't we cutting it a bit close?"

"A hundred men and a cargo ship don't come easy," Wheatley answered gruffly. "Want to see a pile of money disappear? Try moving animals against their will."

Claire noticed a tent with wounded men inside. "What happened?"

"This island happened," Wheatley said grimly. "I've lost five men already." He turned to Owen. "You can thank your *Velociraptor* pal for two of them."

He strode on ahead. Owen gave Claire a look. They were both thinking the same thing.

This isn't going to be easy.

CHAPTER 5

First it was Jurassic Park, then
Jurassic World. What's next?
—Dr. Ian Malcolm

Inside a canvas tent, the team studied a map of the island identical to the one Claire had seen in Eli Mills's office. She put her finger on it. "The only place the tracking system can be activated is here, in the bunker under this radio tower. We get there and we can tap into the main Radio Frequency Identification receiver."

"So how do we get there?" Franklin asked. "Are there secure underground tunnels? I heard all big theme parks have secret underground tunnels."

Wheatley smirked, but Claire said, "Actually, there are *some* tunnels under the park, but none that would get us from here to the bunker. We'll have to drive."

With her finger, she traced a route on the map from their current location to the radio tower. "We'll go down Main Street and through the Gyrosphere Valley."

Franklin handed out tablet computers modified with antennae. "I fitted these tablets with the old park software. They'll be able to track each dinosaur's chip and identify the species once we tap into the system."

"We have capture teams ready to save as many as we can," Wheatley said. "But your Raptor's the one we're worried about. She's slippery. It's like trying to catch a squid with your bare hands."

Owen smiled and shook his head. "You can't catch Blue. We have to just hope she shows herself."

"You think she might do that because of your . . . connection?" Wheatley asked.

"Our auras vibrate at the same frequency," Owen answered. "We synced our biological rhythms over many nights hunting naked under the full moon."

Wheatley just stared at him.

"I'm messing with you, man," Owen confessed

with a grin. "I know what she likes to eat."

VRRRROOOM! A big six-wheeled armored military vehicle pulled up. Covered in heavy protective metal, it was built to drive through explosives.

"I call that one," Franklin said as he moved to enter the massive vehicle.

Claire's team and Wheatley's trackers piled into two armored vehicles and headed out through the security gates in the fence surrounding the base camp. They were followed by a cage truck just large enough for a *Velociraptor*.

In one vehicle, Owen sat between Zia and Claire. Wheatley and three of his trackers cleaned their tranquilizer rifles. Through a window, Zia looked up at a guard in a security tower. His hands were on a huge automatic gun.

Franklin knocked on the inside wall of the vehicle, testing its strength. "The *T. rex*'d be dead by now, right?" he asked, trying to sound casual. "What's the life span?"

"It's impossible to know the maximum life span," Owen said as they rumbled and bounced along. "Especially of a clone in a completely different environment. Take a caveman who would've lived twenty years in his natural environment. Feed him prime meals and give him health care, and he's gonna live five times as long."

That wasn't the answer Franklin wanted to hear. "So," he repeated slowly to himself, "the *T. rex*'d be dead by now, right?"

The caravan of three vehicles made its way into the jungle. Ash fell from the smoking volcano looming in the distance.

They soon reached Jurassic World's old Main Street. Once a place where park visitors took breaks from dinosaur sightseeing and grabbed a bite to eat, or purchased souvenirs for friends and family back home, this relic of happier times was now being swallowed up by the encroaching jungle. Vines climbed over the buildings. Windows were broken. Old merchandise from the gift shop was scattered on the ground.

Claire stared out the reinforced windows of the armored vehicle, remembering the crowds running down this street, screaming and fleeing from the *Pteranodons*. She remembered trying to protect her nephews from the dinosaurs. The *Velociraptors*. The *Tyrannosaurus rex*. The Indominus Rex. The *Mosasaurus*. . . .

"There's a *Brachiosaurus*," Zia exclaimed, "right through those trees!"

As they watched the huge, long-necked vegetarian nibble the leaves at the tops of the trees, Wheatley eyed Claire and Owen. "They're not all so friendly," he said. "Remember?"

Claire and Owen locked eyes. Yes, they remembered.

The caravan passed through Main Street and the scene quickly opened up onto Gyrosphere Valley. The vehicles rolled through the overgrown meadow littered with the bleached bones of dinosaurs that carnivores had picked clean. Broken and abandoned Gyrospheres, glass vehicles that visitors once drove among the giant dinosaurs of Jurassic World, were scattered around the valley floor like the forgotten toys of a giant.

It didn't take much longer for them to reach their target: a bunker dug into a mountain, overlooking the valley. Mounted high above the bunker was a tall, rusted radio tower.

The three vehicles rolled up and parked. Claire's team got out. Claire pointed to an access panel. Franklin patched in his tablet and started trying to get past the security system to open the bunker's door.

As Franklin worked, Owen, Claire, and Zia looked out over the ruined park.

Suddenly, there was a loud rumble, and the earth shook violently!

Franklin yelped and grabbed onto Owen. Claire steadied herself against the bunker wall. Zia just rolled with the tremor.

Wheatley smiled at Franklin's panic. "Easy, tiger. That was a small one."

Turning back to his tablet, Franklin punched in a few final numbers. The bunker doors slowly ground open. "After you, tiger," he said to Wheatley with a wry smile.

Wheatley went inside. Claire and her team followed him. Most of Wheatley's men stayed outside to stand watch, their rifles ready.

It was dusty inside the bunker, which was filled with long-dead computer monitors and radio equipment. Franklin opened a metal cabinet. Inside were hundreds of wires. He found the ones he was looking for and patched his laptop into the system. Here and there, lights blinked on as power began to surge through the long-dormant equipment.

"Are the animals' ID chips still transmitting?" Owen asked. "Wouldn't the batteries be dead by now?"

"The dinosaur *is* the battery," Claire explained. "The transmitters are powered by body heat and the animal's movement." She put her palm against a hand scanner. It lit up, authorizing entry to the system. Turning to Franklin, she asked, "How long will it take you to—"

"I'm in," Franklin said.

Owen raised his eyebrows, impressed. "They could use you at the National Security Administration."

"Applied," Franklin said. "Twice."

"He lacks the interpersonal skills necessary for mainstream employment," Zia explained.

A map of the park appeared on a screen, with dots showing each dinosaur's location. Several were clustered on the island's eastern shore. "Those are the ones we've already caught," Wheatley said. "Eleven species. Can you single out the Raptor?"

"I need a species code," Franklin said.

"D-nine," Owen said without hesitation.

Franklin typed the code into his tablet. All but one of the dots disappeared.

"There she is," Owen said. He turned to Franklin. "Can you make the tracking system portable?"

He handed Owen a tablet. "Already have. I just need to stay logged in here to transmit to your tablets."

"I'm going with you," Zia told Owen. "We don't

know what condition she's in."

"Could get ugly out there, Miss," Wheatley warned.

Zia held up a massive tranquilizer cartridge. "These are powerful sedatives. One too many and she could have respiratory failure. If that happens, you're gonna need me around. Also, I'm not soft and witless like your comment implies."

She strode off, and Owen, amused, started to follow her out. Claire stopped him. "Hey," she said, "be careful."

"If I don't make it back," he said, "remember you're the one who made me come."

She smiled, and he left.

The military vehicle rumbled along the edge of the jungle. Inside, Owen studied his tablet. Blue was close.

"Stop here," he said. "She'll know we're coming no matter what, but I can't get near her in this thing." The vehicle braked to a halt.

"Let's load out," Wheatley said.

Owen led the way into the dense brush. Wearing a medical backpack, Zia followed close behind him. Wheatley and his men brought up the rear. They were on edge and alert, with their tranquilizer rifles ready.

They cautiously approached the partially eaten carcass of a dinosaur. Some carnivore had been feeding there. Recently.

Wheatley gestured toward Owen's tablet with its tracking signal. "Kind of takes the sport out of it."

Owen looked at him. "This isn't my idea of sport."

Behind them, in the dark jungle foliage, something was moving. . . .

"Animal tracking is the *oldest* sport," Wheatley insisted. "It's in our DNA. Aiming. Running. Team sports. Pretty much anything anyone likes to do outdoors goes back to our instinct to hunt."

Zia couldn't believe what she was hearing. "You know we're not *hunting* this animal, right?"

"Hunting, tracking." Wheatley shrugged. "It's all the same."

Owen spotted something in the mud. Raptor tracks. He checked his tablet. Blue's beacon was close. He put the tablet in Zia's backpack. "I'm going on alone."

"Whatever you say," Wheatley said. He'd lost two men to Blue, and he didn't want to be the third.

CHAPTER 6

In the last century, we amassed landmark
technological power, and we've consistently proven ourselves
incapable of handling that power.
—Dr. Ian Malcolm

Back in the bunker, Franklin tapped a dead light
bulb with his finger. It flickered on. "Fixed it," he
announced proudly. It then promptly shorted out and
shattered.

"Stop fixing things," Claire ordered. She checked
her watch, impatient for Owen's and Zia's return.
Franklin collapsed into the rolling chair beside her.

But a beep from his tablet made him sit up.
Owen's beacon on the screen had moved close enough
to Blue's signal to trigger a warning.

"He's close," Claire said.

In the deep jungle, Owen pushed his way through thick brush beneath a dense canopy. It was hot. Insects buzzed. The air was still. Though the sun was shining, the leaves overhead plunged the jungle into shadow.

Owen heard water running over rocks. He pressed forward and found a small creek. After following the stream for a few steps, he came upon a narrow path leading away from the water. Animals must have followed the track to the creek to drink.

He knelt down, checking the path for Raptor tracks. Then he cocked his head.

Owen could feel a pair of eyes watching him. . . .

Standing up slowly, he peered into the jungle, listening carefully. In the dark greenery, something moved. Leaves rustled.

Pretending not to notice, Owen walked farther along the path. At the base of a steep rocky ridge, he came upon a gnarled tree. Under the tree, he found the rusting remains of an old Jurassic Park vehicle, covered in twisting vines. Around the SUV were the gnawed bones of small animals.

Something had been living here. Something that hunted.

There was another movement in the undergrowth. "There you are," Owen said softly. It had to be Blue.

Owen was nervous. He didn't know whether Blue would remember him. *Will she attack?* he thought. *It's been three years. . . .*

With his hands open and stretched forward, he slowly approached the bushes where he'd heard movement. She had to be close. . . .

WHOOSH! A few Compys ran out of the bushes and scampered away. Each *Compsognathus* was about the size of a chicken. Owen exhaled and watched them go quickly.

BAM! Behind him, Blue jumped down from the trees onto the wrecked vehicle! Owen spun around to face her.

"Hey, Blue," he said gently. "You miss me?"

The Raptor hissed and snapped, baring her sharp teeth. If she'd missed him, she didn't seem to be showing it now.

Owen raised his hand and clicked the clicker he had used when training Blue and her siblings. He was signaling that he was the alpha male, the guy in charge. Not someone to be hissed and snapped at.

Blue stared at Owen. Then she gave a low growl.

"Hey!" he said sharply. She stopped growling. "Easy." Owen tried to calm her down. Keeping his eyes on Blue and one hand stretched forward, he reached with his other hand into his bag. "I brought you something."

He held a dead rat up by its tail where Blue could easily see and smell it. "Dead rat. Your favorite." He moved his hand just a little closer, offering her the treat.

But Blue didn't go for it. She seemed suspicious. She snapped her teeth again, keeping her distance. Owen was concerned. *This might not work,* he thought. *If she doesn't take this rat, what am I going to do?*

"Come on, Blue," he urged. "You know me. Take the rat. I swear there's nothing wrong with it."

Blue tilted her head, as though she were considering Owen's words. She sniffed the air. But she was still uncertain. She gave another low growl.

"Eyes on me," Owen commanded. "Right here." Blue looked him right in the eye. "That's it. Good."

Blue stood stock-still for a moment. Then, slowly, she took one small step forward with her right foot. She held that pose for a second. Then she took a small step with her left foot.

Owen held the rat up a little higher. "Come on," he said. "You're okay."

Blue eyed her old trainer warily. She gave one more low, soft growl deep in her throat.

Owen raised his other hand a little, as if to say, "Hey, none of that, now."

Finally, the Raptor came down off the SUV and closed the distance between her and Owen. She was inches away from him. He'd won her trust back.

"Good girl," he said, drawing out the words.

Blue moved her head toward the dead rat dangling by its tail from Owen's fingers. He was about to drop it into her open mouth when—

THHHUKKK! A tranquilizer dart slammed into Blue's flank! She shrieked and bared her teeth!

CHAPTER 7

We've taken things too far.
—Dr. Ian Malcolm

"**H**ey!" Owen yelled. "I said to wait for my signal!"

Wheatley and his trackers emerged from the bushes, their weapons raised and aimed at Blue. It was Wheatley who had shot her with the tranquilizer, unwilling to wait. He had no intention of letting the Raptor get away.

Blue staggered slightly but didn't fall down. She was woozy, but a single dart wasn't enough to knock her out.

"Wheatley, back off!" Owen shouted, furious that his careful approach to Blue had been ruined. How could he ever expect her to trust him after this?

"Don't get angry, now," Wheatley said to Blue, ignoring Owen. He kept aiming his trank rifle right at Blue. "These darts won't hurt you. Just a little prick—like getting your wisdom teeth out."

A bearded tracker fired another dart. But the shot came too late. Blue was already airborne.

The Raptor leapt through the air and landed on the lead tracker, digging her sharp sickle-shaped claw in deep. It stuck in his claw-proof vest, which saved his life . . . but only for a moment, and he knew it. In a near panic, the tracker yanked his sidearm out of its holster. This was no tranquilizer gun. It was a pistol loaded with real bullets.

"NO!" Owen yelled. "Don't shoot!"

BLAM! The bullet hit Blue's leg. She screeched, then opened her mouth wide enough to fit around the man's entire head.

"SHOOT IT!" he screamed. "SHOO—"

CHOMP! In a single powerful bite, Blue took care of the tracker. He wouldn't be bothering her ever again.

But then, *THHHUKKK!* Another dart, fired by Wheatley, hit Blue. She snarled in pain, starting to run toward Wheatley to attack, but just before she reached him, she dropped to the ground, knocked out cold by the tranquilizer.

"You!" Owen couldn't contain his fury. He charged at Wheatley, planning to tackle him to the ground, to punish him for his responsibility in the wounding of Blue and the needless death of the tracker.

Wheatley calmly turned and aimed his tranquilizer gun at Owen.

"Owen, watch out!" Zia yelled.

Owen grabbed one of the trackers and spun him toward Wheatley. *THUKKK!* Wheatley's dart hit his own man right in the chest. The tracker went limp in Owen's arms.

Owen flung the unconscious man aside and drew his own gun. *THUKKK!* Another one of Wheatley's men fired his trank gun at Owen, hitting him in the side. The power of the dart's impact jerked him back. He dropped to his knees, fighting the powerful sedative rushing through his veins. He locked eyes with Wheatley and gave him a burning look full of rage. Wheatley returned his look with a smile of utter contempt as Owen's eyes rolled back in his head and he collapsed to the ground, unconscious. Zia ran to Owen's side and pulled out the dart. Behind her, a trank rifle clicked as Wheatley reloaded. Without hesitating, Zia picked up the unconscious tracker's tranquilizer rifle and aimed it at Wheatley.

At Zia's feet, Owen and Blue lay motionless on the jungle floor, while all around, Wheatley and his men aimed their trank rifles at her.

It was a standoff.

"You shoot, and it'll take four seconds for the tranquilizer to reach my brain," she said, speaking slowly and clearly. "That's plenty of time for me to pull the trigger."

A drop of sweat trickled down Zia's forehead.

"You shoot me," she said, jerking her head toward Blue, "and that animal dies."

Wheatley hesitated. Zia kept the trank gun pointed right at him. "We have doctors," he said. "We don't need you."

"She's losing blood from her gunshot wound," Zia countered. "Without me, you'll never get her back to camp alive."

Wheatley looked down at Blue. He hated to admit it, but Zia was right. The Raptor was bleeding from the wound in her leg where his man had shot her. He needed this dinosaur to live.

He nodded to his men, a single quick lift of his

44

chin. They lowered their weapons. "Keep her alive," he barked at Zia. "Follow my orders. You're to be seen, not heard. Got it?"

Zia lowered her trank rifle and turned to Blue, hoping to stop her bleeding.

Wheatley looked up at the smoking volcano and wiped sweat from his brow. One of the trackers came up to him and spoke softly so Zia couldn't hear. "What about him?" he asked, indicating Owen with a quick move of his head.

Wheatley gave a quick, cold smile. "Leave him. Got your tablet?"

The tracker nodded and pulled out a computer tablet.

"Good," Wheatley said. "Close that door we left open."

In the bunker, Claire clicked the button on her radio. "Owen, can you hear me?" No voice came in return, only static.

"Something happened to them," Claire said, worried.

"If something happened to them," Franklin asked, "what happens to us?"

BOOOOM! Another tremor—stronger, louder, deep in the earth. Dust fell from the ceiling. Claire and Franklin froze.

BOOOOM! A crack spidered up the wall and across the ceiling.

"Nature's angry," Franklin said.

Claire headed down the long corridor toward the open bunker doors to see what was going on outside. Franklin followed her. But as they made their way down the hall, the bunker doors started to close!

"No! Wait!" Claire shouted, running now, with Franklin close behind.

SLAM! The thick doors sealed shut in their faces.

CHAPTER
8

It ain't gonna stop with the de-extinction
of the dinosaurs.
—Dr. Ian Malcolm

After pounding on the heavy door for some time, Claire and Franklin turned around to look back at the dim light of the control room. "What's going on?" Franklin asked. "Why did they close the doors? Are they protecting us?"

"I don't think so," Claire answered.

The earth shook again.

Outside in an armored truck barreling through

Gyrosphere Valley, Wheatley spoke into his satellite phone. "Mission accomplished."

Suddenly, there was an enormous explosion of rock and lava from the volcano! *BOOOM!*

"Just in the nick of time," he added.

The voice on the other end of the line shouted, "What's going on there? We're two days behind schedule already!"

It was Eli Mills, back in Lockwood's mansion. And he did not sound like the smooth, charming man that Claire had met.

"We got the Raptor," Wheatley reported. "So we can start transport now."

"No more delays, you hear me?" Mills barked. "If we don't get those animals—"

"Mr. Mills?" said a small voice.

Mills wheeled around to find Maisie standing at the door to his office. "Not now, Maisie," he said, trying to keep the impatience out of his voice.

"Are the dinosaurs safe?" Maisie asked, but Mills paid her no mind, so she spoke up and asked again, "Are they safe?"

"Not now!" Mills snapped, unable to hide his

anger.

Maisie drew back, frightened by his sudden change. He could see in her eyes that she was thinking of running straight to her grandfather. Mills composed himself. He smiled.

"Sorry, honey, this is an important call," he said. "Go on up to the library and I'll meet you in a few minutes, okay?"

"Okay," Maisie said uncertainly.

"I'll tell you all about it," Mills reassured her. "Promise."

He gave her a big smile. She backed out of the office into the hallway, a little scared of him now. He shut the door behind her and continued his call with Wheatley. "Whatever it takes! Get those animals back now!"

In the jungle, Owen lay flat on the ground, still unconscious.

A low rumble. The earth shook.

Owen opened his eyes. He struggled to rise, but most of his body was still paralyzed from the dart. He was able to lift his head enough to scan the jungle. He saw a line of trees on fire in the distance. The volcano was erupting. This was it.

The shadow of a massive animal passed over him. And then a big, coarse tongue licked his face, leaving streaks of spit.

Owen struggled to move his face away from the wet tongue. He saw its mouth and snout. A massive horn. The animal huffed, drooled, and wheezed.

BOOOM! A deafening rumble from the volcano!

Startled, the animal reared up, lifting its front legs to the sky. It was a *Sinoceratops,* a vegetarian dinosaur that wouldn't eat Owen.

But it could smash him.

Unable to roll out of the way, Owen saw the *Sinoceratops's* gigantic, heavy feet coming down toward him—

WHOMP!!! WHOMP!!! The dinosaur's feet crashed down on either side of Owen's head, just missing him. The *Sinoceratops* ran off, away from the volcano. A stream of molten lava oozed down a nearby hill, scorching everything in its path.

Owen tried to move, fighting the sedative in his body. The lava drew nearer. He clawed the ground. He was starting to feel the heat. Up the hill behind him, more trees caught fire, their trunks bursting into flame one by one.

Finally, summoning all his strength, Owen managed to roll away from the lava. He was getting beyond the burning jungle when—

BAM! He rolled right into a fallen tree.

Somehow he managed to wrench himself over the log, only to face more lava seeping toward him. Surrounded on all sides by the fiery molten rock, he saw the lava swallow the Jurassic World vehicle. It hissed as the metal melted like butter.

With incredible effort, he hauled himself up to his hands and knees, calling on every ounce of his will to move.

Inside the bunker, Claire tried to get reception on her cell phone. Franklin typed away furiously on his tablet, trying to open the doors. It was growing hotter and hotter.

"'Take the job, son. Build your people skills,'" Franklin muttered. "Thanks, Dad."

BEEP BEEP! Franklin jumped at the loud sound.

"Proximity alert," Claire explained. "Something's coming."

They stared at the blinking red dot on the monitor. An animal with an embedded tracking device appeared to be moving through the maze of underground tunnels toward the bunker.

Franklin stared into the dark tunnel behind them. "Where does that lead?"

"It connects with other quadrants of the park," she answered.

"I *knew* there had to be secret tunnels," Franklin said.

BOOM. BOOM.

Something big was coming.

CHAPTER
9

We're causing our own extinction. . . .
—Dr. Ian Malcolm

"**I**t's the *T. rex*," Franklin guessed, horrified.

BOOM.

"It's the *T. rex*, isn't it?" he asked.

"Will you stop?" Claire said, staring down the dark tunnel. "It's not a *T. rex*. Probably."

"Probably!"

They nervously approached the tunnel entrance, waiting to see what would emerge. There was nowhere else for them to go.

Then, behind them, they heard a terrible hiss as hot lava began to seep through cracks in the ceiling! Flaming drips of lava trickled down, burning and sparking. Claire and Franklin spun around to face the falling lava.

From the dark tunnel behind them emerged . . . a *Baryonyx*!

They whipped back around to see the fierce dinosaur. "See?" Claire said. "It's not the *T. rex*!"

"How is this better?" Franklin asked.

He had a point. The *Baryonyx* had a long, narrow mouth full of cone-shaped teeth and looked a little like a crocodile. Except much bigger. And she could also stand on her back legs.

The carnivore stalked them, backing them up against a wall. Suddenly a cascade of lava poured down through a crack in the ceiling, putting a wall of fire between them and the *Baryonyx*.

Claire noticed a circle of light hitting the floor. She looked at the ceiling and saw a long round shaft with a ladder leading up to a hatch portal. She jumped up and pulled at the ladder, but it wouldn't come down.

"It's stuck!" she shouted, looking around wildly and then pointing. "Chair!"

Franklin rushed to grab a chair in the far corner. The *Baryonyx* snapped at him through gaps in the wall of lava. Franklin slid the rolling chair across the floor to Claire, who clambered up onto it. From the chair's height she was able to pull herself up. She hurried up the ladder, followed quickly by Franklin.

"We made it!" Franklin cheered. "Yeah! Go us!"

CLANK! The rusty ladder suddenly dropped down, putting Franklin close to the *Baryonyx*'s reach. The beast snapped at his feet as he scrambled back up the ladder.

At the top of the shaft, Claire tried to turn the hatch wheel, but it was jammed.

ROOOOAAAARR! They could feel the moist breath of the *Baryonyx* rushing up from below as she tried to tear her way up the shaft after them. Working together, Claire and Franklin finally wrenched the hatch open and climbed out into the sunlight. *CLANK!* They slammed the hatch closed, leaving the *Baryonyx* raging in the shaft below.

Safe from the *Baryonyx*, Claire and Franklin caught their breath and looked around to realize they were now standing in the middle of Gyrosphere Valley. Something else caught their eye then, a surprising sight: Owen running toward them! As he approached, Owen shouted, "I'd start running if I were you!" Suddenly, behind him, a stampede of dinosaurs of all shapes and sizes broke through the tree line! The animals were trying to escape the lava and burning forest.

Claire and Franklin turned and ran, too. Owen soon caught up with them.

"Wheatley left us to die," Claire gasped.

"Me too," Owen said.

"Where's Zia?" Claire asked, breathing hard.

"They took her," Owen said as they headed toward the ocean cliff at the base of the sloping valley. It was the only way out.

The three of them sprinted, weaving in and out of stampeding dinosaurs. Before they were trampled, they needed to find a safe spot to wait while the thundering herd passed them by. Claire spotted a Gyrosphere nestled against a fallen tree. "There!" she shouted, pointing.

"Get in!" Owen yelled over the roar. Claire and Franklin dove through the open door of the Gyrosphere. But before Owen could join them, a *Carnotaurus* separated from the stampede and started stalking him around the Gyrosphere. This nightmarish carnivore looked like a *T. rex* but with devilish horns protruding from her forehead. She lunged at Owen, slamming into the glass ball and knocking it loose.

As Owen dove out of the way, the Gyrosphere rolled downhill, its door snapping closed with Claire and Franklin trapped inside!

The *Carnotaurus* turned her attention back to Owen, but then—

ROOOOAAARRR! A massive head snatched the *Carnotaurus* in its jaws, snapped its neck, and dropped the dead carcass like a rag doll. Owen looked up in awe. It was the *T. rex*.

BOOOM! Another explosion from the volcano! The *T. rex* considered Owen for a moment—most likely as an unusual snack. Then she looked back toward the approaching lava flow and ran off toward the ocean.

Owen took off after the Gyrosphere, which was rolling faster and faster downhill with Claire and Franklin trapped inside. "Brakes! Brakes!" Franklin screamed. Claire tried pulling back on the control stick, but it broke off in her hand.

Now they were rolling so fast they started to pass some of the dinosaurs that had passed them earlier.

Claire looked back and saw Owen running after them. Then he was swallowed up by a cloud of black ash.

She looked forward just in time to see the edge of the cliff! The Gyrosphere rocketed off and fell two hundred feet, as Claire and Franklin clung to each other, screaming as they hurtled toward the crashing waves below.

CHAPTER 10

Life is not written on dollar bills. . . .
—Dr. Ian Malcolm

SPLASH! The Gyrosphere plunged into the ocean. Water leaked through the door seams, starting to fill the bubble. Thick legs churned the water as dinosaurs treaded water around them like swimming elephants.

Lava hissed into the ocean. Claire and Franklin tried to open the sinking Gyrosphere's door, but it wouldn't budge. The water rose to their waists as they frantically pushed at the door.

A figure swam down to them—Owen! He tried pulling the door open from the outside, but it was stuck. He pulled out his revolver and tried to fire at the lock, but a drop of lava seared his arm. He dropped his gun, which sank out of sight.

He pulled at the door again, but a dinosaur's tail knocked into him, sweeping him away. The Gyrosphere continued to fill with water. Claire and Franklin took final breaths from the small pocket of air at the top of the sphere. Then they were submerged, frantically kicking at the door.

Owen returned and pulled at the door with all his might while Claire and Franklin tried desperately to hold their breath. Just before it was too late, *WHOOSH!* Owen was able to slide the door to the side! Claire grabbed Owen's outstretched hand, and Franklin followed. They swam to the surface, dodging falling globs of molten lava.

They reached the beach exhausted and collapsed onto the sand, gasping. Then Claire said, "We need to find Zia."

"She'll be with Blue," Owen said. "Can you still track them?"

Franklin lifted his shattered tablet from the surf. "Not anymore."

As Claire lay there thinking about what had happened, she grew more and more angry. They were supposed to have worked together to save the dinosaurs and take them to a sanctuary. Instead, Zia had been captured. Owen had been abandoned. And she and Franklin had been locked in the bunker to die.

"It was a lie," Claire said. "It was *all* a lie!"

"Not all of it," Owen said, looking up.

A helicopter carried a sedated *Stegosaurus* in a hanging cage. It landed near the dock across the bay, where a transport ship was anchored. Men were loading more unconscious dinosaurs onto the ship.

Wheatley walked among the men, barking orders. "Get all this tech on board! We don't leave anything behind!"

He stopped by the *Stegosaurus*. "Hold! Don't have one of these yet." He opened his vest. Inside, it was filled with different sizes of pliers. He chose a pair and approached the sedated *Stegosaurus*.

"Hello, baby," he said, grinning. Reaching through the bars, Wheatley pulled up the dinosaur's lip, grabbed a tooth with his pliers, and yanked it out. "You'll feel that when you wake up."

He opened a bandanna and wrapped the bloody

tooth with others he'd taken from the recently captured dinosaurs, like some sick collection of trophies. Then he jumped onto a passing truck as it drove up a ramp into the boat. Fires were burning through the jungle toward the dock. "Let's go! Let's go!" he shouted.

Claire, Owen, and Franklin watched from nearby. "If they already had the dinosaurs," Franklin asked, "why did they need us?"

"They needed the tracking system to capture Blue," Claire said angrily. Then she spotted Zia next to a cage holding Blue. "There's Zia!"

"We need to get on that boat," Owen said.

Franklin didn't like the idea of rejoining the guys who'd tried to kill them. "What? The rock is good. We're safe on the rock."

"It's the boat or the lava, Franklin," Claire said.

Franklin looked up to see the glowing, red lava beginning to spill over the side of the cliff above and said, "Yeah, boat's good. I'm all about the boat."

In the scramble to escape from the burning island, the workers left behind one truck. Owen, Claire, and

Franklin raced toward it, frantic to drive up the ramp onto the cargo ship before it left.

The wildfire reached a fuel depot. *BOOOOM!* The explosion knocked Franklin off his feet.

"Get us on that ship!" Owen told Claire. She got in the truck as Owen went back for Franklin.

"Franklin, you need to get up!" Owen shouted as ash and embers fell around them.

"I'm not gonna make it," Franklin moaned.

Claire started the truck.

"Hey! HEY!" Owen insisted. "Look at me! Get up!"

Giving it everything he had, Franklin managed to rise to his feet. He and Owen ran to the truck. Owen jumped onto the back bumper and extended a hand to Franklin. As Claire gunned the engine, Franklin grabbed Owen's hand and got pulled into the back.

On the ship, a crewman ordered, "Drop the ramp! Cut it!"

Just as the speeding truck drove into the cargo hold of the ship, the ramp dropped into the water. *SPLASH!*

Claire parked the truck in a line of vehicles and climbed out, looking around, afraid of being discovered. Luckily, the crew members were too busy watching the island burning. She grabbed a baseball cap and pulled it low over her eyes.

She joined Owen and Franklin at the back of the truck. They watched, horrified, as the scorched island slowly crumbled into the ocean, steam rising. Through the smoky sunlight, a *Brachiosaurus* gave a final roar as steam enveloped her. Owen and Claire felt tremendously sad and guilty at not being able to save all the dinosaurs from the volcano's wrath.

The massive cargo doors closed, plunging the hold into darkness.

In Lockwood's library, a serious man, all business, looked at one of the dinosaur dioramas. Eli Mills walked toward the man, smiling warmly.

"Mr. Eversoll," he said, "so nice to meet you in person after all this time."

"Where are the dinosaurs?" Gunnar Eversoll asked, cutting through the pleasantries.

"Oh," Mills said. "There was a bit of a delay. . . ."

"Am I supposed to sell these?" Eversoll asked sarcastically, jerking a thumb toward the fake dinosaurs in the diorama.

"They'll be here," Mills assured him.

Eversoll turned and started to walk away. "I won't deal with amateurs. I'm contacting my buyers and calling it off." He pulled out his cell phone and started to make a call.

Panicking a bit, Mills followed after him. "No, wait. The animals will be here tomorrow. Thirty-seven, all told. Your clients won't be disappointed. Eleven different species. I estimate they'll fetch at least eight million dollars per species."

Eversoll snorted. "Eight million dollars is a slow Tuesday in my business. You're wasting my time. I'm shutting it down." He tapped on his phone again.

"No, wait," Mills said urgently. "Let me show you something." He gestured toward the dioramas. "All this is the past. I want to talk about the *future*."

Eversoll looked at him impatiently. "I'll give you ten minutes."

Mills led him to an elevator and punched a code into a control pad. From the balcony above, Maisie watched, memorizing the code. The doors opened, and the two men took the elevator down.

"The sale of the Isla Nublar dinosaurs is to finance our future operations," Mills explained. "It's seed money. Just the prelude to something much more ambitious."

"And lucrative, I trust," Eversoll replied.

When the elevator doors opened, Mills and Eversoll stepped into a huge, gleaming underground lab. "If our history has taught us anything," Mills continued, "it's that man is inevitably drawn to war. And that he'll use any means to win."

Eversoll realized what Mills was suggesting. "You're going to weaponize the dinosaurs?"

Mills gave a slight smile, sensing that he'd caught Eversoll's interest. "We've used animals in combat for centuries. Elephants. Horses. The Soviets used disease-bearing rats against troops in Stalingrad."

He stepped over to a display and activated a revolving hologram of the Indominus Rex. "Our geneticists have created a direct descendant of Dr. Henry Wu's masterpiece. . . ."

"The Indominus Rex," Eversoll finished, staring at the hologram.

"Highly intelligent," Mills said. "Unprecedented sense of smell. Every bone and muscle designed for hunting and killing."

He nodded toward a glass case that held the

invaluable Indominus Rex bone recovered from the bottom of the Jurassic World lagoon. "Her DNA, retrieved from the island, provided the architecture for the new design. We call it the Indoraptor in honor of its illustrious heritage," Mills said proudly.

Greed lit up Eversoll's eyes. "Show it to me."

CHAPTER 11

I'm talking about man-made cataclysmic change.
—Dr. Ian Malcolm

Mills led Eversoll down a metal spiral staircase. The lower level was full of steel cages built into cement walls.

"The world's superpowers have drones in the sky, underwater, and underground," Mills said. "Their enemies have no choice but to respond. This animal is vicious, relentless, and expendable."

As they walked down a long corridor, Eversoll felt nervous, despite the heavy bars on the cages. From one dark cage came a scraping sound.

"The proceeds of tomorrow's sale will fund our final round of development," Mills continued. "Once we've ironed out the character flaws, we'll breed them for use in the field."

"Character flaws?" Eversoll asked, looking concerned.

"Genetic design is trial and error," Mills said with a slight shrug. "Mostly error."

Through the bars, Eversoll could make out a shadowy animal in the dark cage. The animal was ten feet tall and sleek. Eversoll could hear it breathing quietly.

"Why's it so dark in there?" Eversoll asked.

Mills smiled. "The light in the cell burned out. We used two tranquilizing darts to put the Indoraptor down. The technician went into the cage." He paused and looked at Eversoll. "And that's when we learned it takes *three* darts to put it down."

A shaft of light in the cage showed that the Indoraptor was using its long claw to toy with a human skull. That was the scraping sound he'd heard.

"But the really interesting part," Mills continued, "is that when we reviewed the security tapes, we saw that the Indoraptor had *purposely* broken the light. It was hungry."

A low growl came from inside the cage. The Indoraptor flicked the skull against the bars. *Clink.*

"Oh, I wouldn't stand there," Mills warned Eversoll. He looked down and saw that his feet were on a line of red tape. He quickly took a step back.

"We need to show this thing to the buyers," Eversoll said, excited.

The Indoraptor growled.

In the cargo hold of the transport ship, two dozen trucks with steel cages on their beds were lined up. The cages held sedated dinosaurs. Blue, in pain from her gunshot wound, moaned.

"Shut that thing up!" barked a guard with a flashlight.

Inside the truck, Zia stroked Blue's neck. "Shh. Easy, now." The Raptor was restrained and muzzled. The canvas flaps at the back of the truck opened. Claire, Owen, and Franklin climbed in. "You're alive!" Zia exclaimed. "How did you get—"

Owen put a finger to his lips and crouched down beside Blue.

"Who are all these guys?" Zia whispered, indicating

the men on the ship.

"Animal traffickers," Owen said. "I've seen cages like this before. It's all left over from the ivory trade. They're gonna sell the dinosaurs."

Zia shook her head. "Not Blue. They want her for something else, I think. But if I don't have clean instruments—"

Blue screeched in pain. The bandage on her leg was red.

"She's hemorrhaging," Zia said. She put Claire's hand over the wound. "Steady pressure." She then turned to Owen and said, "She's losing blood fast. We need to get the bullet out."

"You left it in?" Franklin asked, sounding shocked.

"I'm sorry, are you a doctor?" Zia asked him, annoyed by his implication that she didn't know what she was doing. She flicked a syringe and injected an anesthetic. The ship rolled, going over a wave. Blue moaned.

"Hey, Blue," Owen said, trying to comfort her. "Shh . . . shh . . ."

"I can't extract the bullet without a blood transfusion," Zia said. "Which one of you knows how to find a vein?"

"I used to do blood drives for the Red Cross," Claire volunteered.

"Great," Zia said. "You're gonna put an intravenous catheter into the external jugular, like this one." She pointed out the jugular vein on Blue's neck. "Don't miss. Franklin, take over for Claire."

She grabbed Franklin's hand and put it on Blue's bleeding wound. He did not look happy about this. Zia turned back to Owen and Claire.

"All the animals on this ship are sedated," she explained. "We need to be at least close on blood type. Look for a carnivore with two or three fingers. No more than three. I think there's only one of them on board. Got it?"

Making their way silently from truck to truck, Owen and Claire soon found the only dinosaur on board that matched Zia's description. . . .

The *Tyrannosaurus rex.*

She lay flat on a slab, locked down by heavy bars. She was sedated, but not completely asleep. Her head was enormous.

Owen nodded to Claire encouragingly. She gently placed her hand on the *T. rex*'s neck. "Easy," she murmured. "We're not gonna hurt you."

The *T. rex* growled a deep, low growl.

"Be good," she said. "There. See? We're friends."

Claire smiled at Owen, amazed and amused at her own attempt to make friends with a *T. rex*. He ran his hand along the dinosaur's neck until he found the jugular vein. "Got it."

Claire nodded.

Owen handed Claire the huge syringe with a tube and a bag attached. She reached to where Owen's hand was, but couldn't follow the jugular vein all around the *T. rex*'s gigantic neck. "I can't feel it," she whispered.

Owen took her hand and moved it onto the vein. "It's right here. Like a throbbing *boom-BOOM*. There."

The *T. rex* moaned. Owen looked at the position of her head and her neck. "Okay," he decided. "You need to climb up there."

Claire looked at him as though he'd lost his mind. "I am not climbing up on a *T. rex*'s back!"

"You'll be fine," Owen reassured her. "It's like riding a bull."

"I didn't grow up in a rodeo or wherever you came from!"

The *T. rex* snorted, loud as a car backfiring. Owen

beckoned for Claire to move.

Her face became determined. Pulling herself up with her arms, Claire climbed onto the dinosaur's back. "Okay," she said. "I did it. I'm on the *T. rex*." She couldn't believe it.

"Good job," Owen congratulated her. "You're making this look normal."

Claire ran her fingers along the vein and tapped the spot where she thought the syringe should go. "There?" Owen nodded. She tried to insert the needle, but the dinosaur's skin was too thick. She tried again, but still couldn't puncture her hide. "I can't get the needle in!"

"Don't worry," Owen said. "She's asleep."

Claire raised the syringe and slammed the needle in. Blood flowed into the tube. The *T. rex* made a loud, huffing sound.

"Shh," Owen said. "Easy, girl . . ."

Suddenly the *T. rex* swung her head, pinning Owen tight against the side of the container! The *T. rex*'s eye slowly opened. Owen's face was right next to the gigantic eyeball. He could see his own reflection in it.

"You okay down there?" Claire asked.

"Mmm-hmm," Owen managed to say.

Outside the container, a passing guard noticed the open door. He slammed it shut—*CLANG!*—and locked the door.

Inside, the loud clang roused the *T. rex*. She began to fully wake up, much to Claire's and Owen's alarm. "Stay there!" Claire whispered to Owen.

"Okay," he said, unable to move.

Claire pulled the full blood bag free and stood up on the *T. rex* as she shifted under her. Jumping up to the container's roof, she squeezed herself through its opening.

The *T. rex*'s eye focused on Owen, glaring. The dinosaur snapped at him, but in the tight quarters of the cage, the predator wasn't quite able to reach him with her teeth. So she tried to slash him with the claws on her back leg. Owen dodged the attack, but he still remained trapped, and the *T. rex* was growing angrier.

Claire leapt down from the top of the container, unlocked the door, and opened it.

For Owen, there was only one path to the door: through the *T. rex*'s jaws.

As the most powerful predator in the world opened her mouth wide, Owen dove. *SNAP!* The sharp teeth just missed him, and he tumbled through the door and out onto the deck. Claire shut the door and locked it. They both were breathing hard.

"Did you see that?" Owen asked. Claire nodded. "Please tell me you got the blood."

She lifted the full bag, showing him. They both smiled.

In Lockwood's mansion, Maisie slipped into her grandfather's bedroom. He was in bed with his eyes closed, but when he heard Maisie, he opened them. "Maisie, what are you doing up?"

"There was a man here today. With Mr. Mills." She frowned. "I didn't like him."

He patted her hand. "I'm sure it was some business about the sanctuary. Nothing for you to worry about."

Maisie shook her head vigorously. "No! They're going to sell the dinosaurs! They're bringing them here!"

For an instant, a shadow crossed Lockwood's face. But he hid his concern, saying, "I'm sure you misunderstood. The animals are on their way to the sanctuary right now."

Maisie looked her grandfather right in the eyes. "I know what I heard."

"It's late," Lockwood sighed. "Why don't we talk about it in the morning?" He kissed her head and gave her a hug.

But on his face was a look of anger and betrayal.

CHAPTER
12

How many times do you have to see the evidence? How many times must the point be made?
—Dr. Ian Malcolm

Zia started the transfusion of *T. rex* blood into Blue's vein. Claire applied pressure to the Raptor's wound, taking over for Franklin, who was grateful to be replaced.

"Owen, restrain her leg so we can get in there," Zia said. "Claire, swab the wound when you can."

Owen tethered Blue's leg. Zia inserted a probe into her wound.

"What's that for?" Franklin asked, grimacing.

"Since we don't have X-rays," Zia explained, "this is the only way to find the bullet."

"You've done this before, right?" Franklin asked.

"Yes," Zia said. "Shh."

"With a live animal?"

She shot Franklin a glance. "We operated on scale models at school. There aren't many actual dinosaurs running around Syracuse, New York." The probe hit something. "There it is!"

Zia slowly pulled out the probe and measured the distance from the bullet hole to Blue's upper thigh, where the bullet had lodged. Then she prepared a lethal dose of anesthesia in a syringe.

"What's that for?" Franklin asked.

"Their bones are hollow," Zia answered. "If the bullet struck a bone, there's nothing we can do. We'll have to put her down."

"In that case, I'll do it," Owen said firmly.

Zia used a scalpel to cut down to the bullet. "Lot of muscle tissue," she murmured. The others watched, tense. Had the bullet hit the bone?

"Okay, here we go," Zia said, picking up the forceps. She steadied her hand, reached in, and pulled out the bullet. It was intact.

Zia exhaled and peered at the incision.

"It missed the bone," she announced. "She's going to be fine."

They all smiled, relieved. Blue shifted gently, waking up.

"Shh! Blue!" Owen said, calming her. "Shh. Easy. It's okay, girl. We got you. We got you."

Under Owen's touch, Blue calmed down.

Early the next morning, Maisie snuck to the keypad beside the service elevator and punched the code she'd memorized by watching her grandfather. The door opened, and she got in.

Down in the lab, she stared at all the displays and equipment. She'd never known all this was down here. Drawn to a video monitor with a baby *Velociraptor* on the screen, she smiled and pressed the play button.

On the screen, Owen was in a pen with four baby Raptors: Echo, Delta, Charlie, and Blue. "Eyes on me," Owen said.

The little Raptors followed the piece of beef jerky in his hand, moving their heads in unison. Owen moved the treat closer. One Raptor snapped at it.

"No." Owen corrected. "Delta, no."

As he tossed treats to the three other Raptors, Delta hissed. "You know the rules," Owen said. "Come on. Play nice, ladies."

The video cut to a shot of Owen speaking directly to the camera. "Day 148. We're experimenting with socializing the Raptors. They've formed a protective unit, like a wolf pack, so when they sense weakness or injury, they assume dominance."

Maisie watched, fascinated, as the video showed Owen pretending to be injured. The baby Raptors instantly attacked, climbing all over him. He shook them loose, noting that Blue seemed to be hanging back a little bit.

"Day 187," Owen said into the camera. "Exciting breakthrough today. I'm pretty sure one of the Raptors is showing high-level socialized behavior."

The video showed Owen working separately with young Blue. He pretended to be injured, but Blue didn't instantly attack. She watched. Then she approached, looking concerned.

"Her name's Blue," Owen's voice narrated. "This one's special. Look at that. She's concerned for me. Her head's tilting. She's craning forward. There's increased eye movement. That's empathy, like you'd see in a mammal. We weren't sure Raptors would ever be capable of this level of bonding. . . ."

As she watched Owen on the video, Maisie smiled. She liked this man.

Now he showed young Blue that he wasn't really hurt. "Hey, I'm all right, Blue. See? Just fine. I'm great." Blue relaxed and looked at him. There clearly was a connection between the man and the dinosaur.

"I have something special," Owen said on the video. "Just for you, pal." He reached into his pack. Blue looked alert. He pulled out a dead rat. Blue grabbed it and ran off happily.

Behind Maisie, a man's voice said, "You sure she'll live?"

Someone was coming!

CHAPTER
13

Change is like death. You don't know what it
looks like until you're standing at the gates.
—Dr. Ian Malcolm

Maisie shut off the video and hid. Mills and another man came out of an office.

"We have blood samples if the Raptor dies," Mills replied.

Dr. Henry Wu looked angry. "That's not good enough. The Raptor is a *behavioral specimen*. We need her in good health."

"What do you want me to do, Henry?" Mills snapped. "*I* didn't shoot her!"

Wu stopped and gave Mills an exasperated look. "You don't have the least understanding of what I'm doing here. Do you see the complexity of creating an *entirely new life form*?"

"I see the complexity of paying for it," Mills countered.

Maisie wanted out of the lab. She spotted the spiral stairs leading down to the dinosaur containment cells. She sneaked toward them. Just then, Wu pivoted and strode toward the stairs. Mills followed him. Maisie hurried down ahead of them.

"All your money will have been wasted if I don't get Blue here in good health," Wu said as he headed down the stairs, his shoes clanking on the metal steps. "To get the next iteration under control, it needs to form a *familial bond* with a closely related genetic link."

"English, Henry," Mills said.

"It needs a *mother*," Wu stated plainly. "Blue's DNA will be part of the next Indoraptor's makeup. So it will be genetically coded to recognize her authority and assume her traits. Empathy. Obedience. Everything the one you have now is missing."

"And how long is that going to take?" Mills asked, following him down the stairs.

"Science is rarely a sprint, Mr. Mills," Wu replied. "It's a marathon."

Maisie reached the bottom of the stairs and looked for a place to hide.

"A marathon sounds expensive," Mills said. He and Wu were almost to the bottom of the stairs. Maisie hurried into a dim corridor.

The one that led to the Indoraptor.

"You must remember this is all uncharted territory," Wu argued. "A wolf, genetically, is barely distinguishable from a bulldog. Within that gray area is . . . art."

Maisie kept backing down the corridor, retreating from the men, unaware of the genetic monster at the other end of the hall.

"I'm just asking if you can do it," Mills said sharply.

Wu looked at Mills coldly. "I can do it."

The two men strode off in opposite directions.

Maisie heard a rattling sound behind her. She peered into the darkness, frightened but curious. She could hear something sniffing, as though it was trying to pick up her scent. She turned and looked down the hallway to see if the men were coming.

A scaly black arm stretched through the bars, its

long, sharp talons reaching—

Maisie took a step forward. The claws came down, combing through her hair. She wheeled around, startled, and found herself face to face with the Indoraptor. He growled, eyeing her. Frozen in fear, Maisie stared into his piercing, predatory eyes.

Someone grabbed her arm. Maisie screamed.

It was Mills. He angrily hauled Maisie up to her room and locked her in.

At night, the cargo ship carrying the dinosaurs arrived at a dock near Lockwood's estate. Owen, Claire, Franklin, and Zia were in the back of the truck holding Blue.

Claire heard the sounds of arrival. "We're here."

"Where?" Franklin asked.

Before she could answer, they heard someone open the driver's door of the truck and climb in. It was Wheatley. He slid open the hatch between the cab and the back compartment to ask Zia about Blue. "Got a heartbeat?"

"Yeah," Zia answered coldly. "Do you?"

He scowled. "I need blood samples."

"Take your own samples," Zia said defiantly.

Wheatley's mouth tightened. He shook his head and closed the hatch. Zia gave Owen, Claire, and Franklin an urgent look that said "Get out of here right away."

Owen and Claire slipped out of the back of the truck and around the side. But just as Franklin was climbing out, a crewman rounded the corner and spotted him.

"What are you doing?" the crewman barked.

Franklin stared. He couldn't think of a lie.

Zia stuck her head out the back of the truck. "I needed a second pair of hands. He volunteered."

The crewman eyed Franklin suspiciously. "Deck crew?"

Franklin searched his brain for the answer a real worker on a ship might give, and "Aye, aye!" was the best he could come up with.

The crewman looked him over skeptically for a brief moment before saying, "Come on. We're loading out. Follow me."

Franklin's eyes widened. "You mean we're leaving the ship? Right now?"

The crewman stopped and stared at Franklin.

"That's what 'loading out' means," he said sarcastically. "Get moving. Come on!"

He turned and walked away. After hesitating for a second, Franklin had no choice but to follow him, trying to pass himself off as some kind of worker on the ship. From underneath the truck where they were hiding, Claire and Owen watched his feet go.

Franklin was not happy. . . .

"Wait here," Owen told Claire. "I'll get Franklin."

But before he could go, the truck's engine started, followed by the engines of all the other vehicles in the ship's cargo hold. Owen realized they *both* needed to get out from under the truck. "Go!" he said.

They scrambled up and hurried back to the truck they'd originally driven onto the ship. They got in, and Owen started the engine. "We'll get Franklin and Zia back," he reassured Claire. "Don't worry."

Claire peered out the truck's window. "Where are we?"

The caravan of trucks carrying dinosaurs rolled down a ramp onto a World War II–era military dock, long abandoned. They drove away from the coast, uphill into a foggy redwood forest, on their way to the Lockwood Estate.

Lockwood lay in his bed, hooked up to an IV drip. As he glared at Mills, he looked weak but very angry. "Did you think you would get away with it? In my own house? Why would you do this, Eli? I've always treated you well."

Mills looked at him coldly. "You entrusted me to guide your fortune into the future. I have."

"Pick up that phone," Lockwood said, nodding toward a telephone beside the bed. "Call the police. It's easier if it comes from you."

Looking as though he was accepting his punishment, Mills reached for the phone. But then his hand went past it. "I'm not the only guilty one here, am I?"

His hand continued to Lockwood's morphine drip. He turned the dial up to a lethal dose, and then looked away from the dying man.

Mills had locked Maisie's door as he was leaving her room. With him gone, Maisie looked out the window, thinking about her grandfather. She could see the headlights of the truck caravan moving in the valley below the mansion. She wiped away her tears and got a determined look on her face.

She found a hairpin and a piece of paper. She slid the piece of paper under the door and positioned it below the lock. Then she pushed the hairpin through the keyhole until the key on the other side of the door fell onto the paper. She carefully pulled the paper into the room, picked up the key, and unlocked the door.

But when she opened the door a crack and peeked out into the hall, she saw a guard Mills had posted near her room. She silently closed the door. Then she turned and looked at her window. It was the only way out.

Owen drove the truck through the woods, following the other trucks. Ahead, they saw elaborate metal gates. "I've been here," Claire said. "This is Lockwood Estate."

"Lockwood must have an awfully big garage," Owen said, thinking of all the vehicles in the caravan.

A man waved them through the gates, but as they passed, he recognized Owen and Claire from the island. He was one of Wheatley's men.

He urgently spoke into his walkie-talkie.

The trucks ahead had reached the mansion and unloaded the dinosaurs into underground containment cells, which lined a vast subterranean facility located beneath the estate. An *Ankylosaurus* limped out into her cramped concrete quarters. There was some hay on the floor. A trough held carrots and celery. The *Ankylosaurus* roared angrily. Other dinosaurs wailed and growled.

In Blue's truck, Zia checked the Raptor's eyes with a flashlight. Blue woke up and kicked one leg free of its restraint. Zia was happy to see her recovering from her surgery so well.

The truck stopped at the top of a ramp. Wheatley jumped out and greeted Mills. "The hunter-warrior has returned with meat for the fire," he said, grinning.

Mills wasn't amused. "Show me."

Wheatley led him around to the back of the truck and pulled the canvas flap open. Mills saw Blue . . . and Zia.

"Who is she?" he asked accusingly.

"We needed a vet," Wheatley explained.

"I want sanitized tools and chemicals to disinfect her wound," Zia said bluntly.

Mills looked at Blue's wound, expertly treated by Zia. Wheatley closed the canvas flap.

"Give her what she needs," Mills said.

"What about what *I* need?" Wheatley asked.

Mills shot him a look. "You'll get your money if the animal lives." He strode off. Wheatley pounded the back of the truck and it drove off toward the containment cells.

Owen and Claire's truck was near the back of the caravan, which had come to a stop. Claire looked at a dark crossroad. "There's a town twenty miles from here."

Owen followed her gaze to the road and said, "We could go get help. Shut this whole operation down."

He thought about it for a moment, then turned the steering wheel, pulling out of the line of trucks. But when he started to turn onto the crossroad, he saw three armed men pointing their guns at them. He hit the brakes.

Out of nowhere, Wheatley stuck his arm through the truck's window and pressed a gun to Owen's temple. "You should have stayed on the island and taken your chances with the volcano. Better odds."

Wheatley and his men took Owen and Claire to one of the concrete containment cells meant for dinosaurs and locked them in. Through the cell's metal bars, they could see the mother *Triceratops* and her baby in the opposite cell. The pair huddled together, and the mother moaned.

"Claire . . . ," came a voice through the bars.

She turned and saw Mills. He said, "You have to let me apologize. I had no intention of bringing you into this. He insisted we have the Raptor—"

Claire lunged at him! Owen held her back, but she still managed to deliver a few solid boot-kicks to the bars. *CLANG! CLANG!*

"So this is it, huh?" Owen asked Mills. "I mean, you're a smart guy. You could probably start a foundation. Cure cancer. But instead you, what? Sell endangered species?"

"These animals were going to die," Mills countered. "I saved their lives."

This made Claire furious. "You betrayed a dying man! For money!"

Mills's eyes turned cold. He stepped closer to the bars. "I admire your idealism, Claire. But we both exploited these creatures. At least I have the integrity to admit it."

"I've never—" Claire started to protest.

"You authorized the creation of the Indominus Rex," he snapped. "You sold a living thing, in a cage, for money. How is it different?" He turned to Owen. "And you. The man who proved Raptors can follow orders. You never thought about the applications of your research? How many millions a *trained predator* might be worth? You two . . . you're the parents of the new world."

BAM! Claire punched Mills right in the mouth through the bars!

He stumbled back, holding his bleeding lip. Wheatley laughed almost good-naturedly and offered Mills his bandanna.

"How do you want to end this?" Wheatley asked Mills. "As far as anyone knows, these two burned up on Isla Nublar."

"Leave them here," Mills said, walking away. "By sunrise they'll have the place to themselves."

Maisie opened her bedroom window and crouched on the sill, looking down to the ground two stories below. She took a deep breath and stepped out onto a stone ledge. As she carefully moved along the ledge, she saw long black cars driving up to the mansion.

Mills and Eversoll stood at the entrance to greet the buyers as they arrived for the dinosaur auction. Eversoll, who'd done business with the buyers before, whispered details about each man as he walked up the stone stairs to the front door.

As one man walked by, Eversoll said, "Development representative for Aldaris Pharmaceuticals." Then he continued as more men passed. "Proxy for Gregor Aldrich, Slovenian arms dealer. Consultant to the Saudi royal family. Horse buyer for Rand Magnus, the oil magnate from Houston—"

"What's his interest?" Mills asked. They weren't selling horses.

"Strictly personal," Eversoll said. "His kid wants a baby *Triceratops*." He greeted the horse buyer with a friendly handshake. "Glenn! How's Janet?"

Someone slammed a car door. Up on the ledge, Maisie was startled and slipped! She regained her footing, but a tiny plastic *T. rex* fell out of her pocket onto the flagstones below.

Eversoll took a Russian mobster aside and spoke to him confidentially. "Listen, you don't get what you want, come see me. I'll pull something from the back." He switched to Russian. "I know what you want, Anton."

"You never disappoint me, Gunnar!" Anton answered in Russian. "Let's have some fun!" He went inside.

Eversoll turned to Mills. "He's only interested in carnivores. Wants two of them."

"Why?" Mills asked.

"Cage match. Five thousand dollars a seat and pay-per-view."

Mills noticed Maisie's plastic dinosaur by his feet. He looked up at the house but saw nothing unusual.

"They're hungry," Eversoll said, smiling. "I can tell. Lockwood's going to have a very good night. Will he be joining us?"

"Unlikely," Mills answered. He checked his watch. By now, the morphine should have done its work. But he had to be sure. "Excuse me."

He went inside.

Maisie pulled herself over a stone wall onto the roof. She ran across to a window. Through it she could see her grandfather sleeping in his big four-poster bed. She raised the window and climbed through, dropping onto the floor and running to her grandfather's side.

"Wake up, Grandfather, wake up!" she said.

There was no response.

"Grandfather, get up!" she pleaded, grabbing his sleeve. "You have to see!"

Maisie shook his arm. He stayed still.

And then she understood.

She fell silent.

She didn't know what to do. Where to go.

CREAK. She heard footsteps in the hallway. She looked back at the open window on the other side of the room, but realized she couldn't get out before the person came in. The bedroom doorknob turned.

CHAPTER
14

Too many lines have been crossed. Genetic
power has been unleashed . . . which of course
is going to be catastrophic.
—Dr. Ian Malcolm

Maisie bolted to the dumbwaiter in the wall
near the bed. She managed to scramble in and slide
the door shut before the person came into the room.
Through a tiny crack in the dumbwaiter door she saw
Mills enter.

He stood there for a moment, looking across
at Lockwood's body, certain that the overdose
of morphine had killed the sick old man. Then he
crossed to the medical equipment next to the bed.

He flipped a switch, and the equipment hummed to life. A monitor lit up, casting a green glow. The heart monitor showed a flat line—no heartbeat.

He thought he heard a noise in the room. He cocked his head, listening.

Mills turned and walked toward the part of the room the noise had seemed to come from. The only thing there was the dumbwaiter in the wall. He slid open the small door.

Empty.

In the dinosaur containment cell, Owen struggled to pick the lock with the multipurpose pocket tool he always carried with him. No matter what he tried, he couldn't get the lock to spring open.

Claire looked past him through the bars at the dinosaurs imprisoned all around them. An *Allosaurus* slowly stood, unable to reach her full height under the concrete ceiling. The dinosaur was cramped in her cell, but Claire still thought she looked beautiful and majestic.

"Do you remember the first time you saw a dinosaur?" she asked.

Owen paused a moment in his attempt to pick the lock. Though he didn't answer, she could tell by the look on his face that he did remember that moment.

"The first time you see them," she said, "it's like a miracle. You've read about them in books and seen their bones in museums, but they're still like myths. You don't really believe they could've existed. And then you see your first one alive, moving, looking back at you. It's . . . breathtaking. I just wanted to help bring that feeling to more people. I never—"

"I know," Owen interrupted. "It's not your fault."

"But it is."

"No. This one's on me. I showed them the way. I trained the Raptors."

Claire looked at him. "Would you have come if it weren't me asking?"

Owen pulled another tool out of his pocket device and tried fitting it into the lock. "Look," he said, "we'll talk about it later, okay?"

"If there *is* a later," Claire replied matter-of-factly.

"There will be," Owen said confidently. "I've got a cabin to finish."

Claire smiled. "You gonna have a hammock? I love a hammock."

"Sorry, hammock's for the dog," he said. "But I'll consider getting a second one. Maybe."

From the next cell came a loud, low groan. *OOORRROOOAAHH!*

"What was that?" Claire asked.

OOROOOGHHUNH! Another groan, followed by the sound of something big stirring in the straw on the floor and then slowly standing up.

"Whatever it is, it's alive," Owen said. He stopped trying to pick the lock on their cell's door and walked over to the wall where the sounds had come from. Looking up, he saw a small, metal-barred opening between their cell and the next. He jumped up, grabbed the bars, and pulled himself up so he could see into the next cell.

The cell was identical to theirs: concrete with steel bars. But the floor was lined with straw, and there was a trough with hay, carrots, and other vegetables. The cell's occupant was ignoring the food, pacing back and forth, huffing angrily.

"Well, look who just woke up!" Owen said.

It was a *Stygimoloch*—Stiggy for short. The herbivore was compact and built like a linebacker. There were short horns over her nose, and spikes sticking out from the back of her head. But the first thing anyone noticed about a Stiggy was her dome-shaped skull. It rose high above her eyes, like the crown of a bald man's head. Owen knew that the skull's bone could be up to nine inches thick. Stiggy liked to butt her unbreakable skull into an attacker's body.

And that gave Owen an idea.

He let go of the bars and dropped back down to the floor. Then he smiled at Claire and said, "We're getting out of here."

In an underground luxury garage, chairs were set up for the dinosaur auction. Buyers filed in and took their seats. Eversoll stood beside a large concrete platform fitted with heavy rails leading to a wide steel door.

"Gentlemen," Eversoll said. "No photographs, please. All sales are final. Let us begin."

In their cell, Owen gave a loud, sharp whistle. The *Stygimoloch* didn't like the high-pitched sound. It turned and rammed the wall between the two cells with its bony head. *THUUUNNK!*

"What are you *doing*?" Claire asked Owen.

"Escaping," he explained.

He whistled again, and Stiggy slammed into the wall again. *THUUUNNNK!*

"You sure about this?" Claire asked.

CHAPTER 15

It's as if we have been genetically designed
to repeat our worst mistakes.
—Dr. Ian Malcolm

In the garage, the auction was under way. A large, steel door at the back of the stage rose, revealing an *Ankylosaurus* in a cage. "Bidding starts at four million," Eversoll announced.

In seconds the bids had reached eight million. And the bids kept coming. Eversoll's eyes lit up. Mills watched in the background, thrilled.

BANG! Eversoll brought down his gavel, ending the bidding auction. "Sold!" Eversoll called. "To the gentleman from Indonesia for eleven million."

A guard pulled a lever. The *Ankylosaurus*'s cage backed out of the room. Out on a loading dock, the cage rolled into a truck. A man shut the back door and locked it. The truck revved, and it drove off into the night.

Another cage was rolled into the garage for the auction. This one held a juvenile *Allosaurus*.

Mills and Eversoll had planned to start the bidding at four million again, but they'd learned from the auctioning of the *Ankylosaurus*. Why start low? "Bidding will start at eight million," Eversoll said. Almost immediately, he got bids of ten million, eleven million, twelve. . . .

THUUUNNNK!!! Stiggy slammed her skull into the concrete. Fragments crumbled from the ceiling. She had almost broken through.

"Stand back," Owen warned.

"Believe me," Claire said, "I will."

He whistled again. *SMASH!* Stiggy crashed through into their cell, disoriented, coughing on dust. But she quickly got herself set to fight. She stared at Claire, who was backed up against the wall.

The dinosaur prepared to charge.

"Uh, Owen?!"

He whistled one more time, and Stiggy wheeled on him. Owen stood right in front of the cell's door. Stiggy charged at him, but Owen grabbed the bars in the door and swung himself up at the last moment. *WHAM!* Stiggy broke through the door.

Out in the corridor between cells, the dinosaur realized she was free. She brayed, setting off roars from the other dinosaurs. Then she ran down the hall, disappearing around a corner.

"You're welcome!" Owen called after it.

In the distance, Stiggy brayed again.

Claire and Owen hurried out of the cell and headed down the corridor. As they passed a dim hallway, Claire noticed movement. She found the door to a dumbwaiter, slightly open. She gently opened the door. Maisie was crouched inside, crying.

"Lockwood's granddaughter," Claire told Owen.

"Hey there," Owen said. "Looks like you could use a friend. You want to come out?"

Maisie shook her head. Claire squatted down to get on the girl's level. "My name's Claire," she said. "Do you remember me?" Maisie nodded. "What's your name?"

"Maisie."

"Maisie, this is Owen."

"I saw you on the video," Maisie said. "With the one called Blue."

"You like dinosaurs?" Owen asked. She nodded. "Come on out. I'll tell you all about Blue, okay?"

She carefully climbed out of the dumbwaiter.

"Wow," Owen said. "You made it all the way down here. You must be pretty brave."

Claire brushed the hair out of Maisie's eyes. "We need to find your grandfather. Can you take us to him?"

Maisie shook her head, and started crying again. She suddenly flung herself into Owen's arms and hugged him desperately. Surprised, Owen tried to comfort her. "Shh, we got you. We got you. Don't worry. . . ."

Claire watched Owen hug Maisie. She liked this gentle side of him.

"How about we just find our friends and get out of here?" Owen asked. Maisie nodded in agreement.

In the garage, the auction was bringing in millions of dollars. Eversoll and Mills were thrilled. Dr. Wu watched disapprovingly. A *Stegosaurus* went for twenty-one million dollars.

Just above, Owen and Claire pressed their way through a tight service tunnel full of pipes and electrical conduits, followed by Maisie. They could hear Eversoll's voice. Following the sound of it, they found a grate in the wall. Through the grate, they could see everything going on in the garage below them. The caged *Stegosaurus* was rolled back out of the room. Owen ran to a window to see where it was going.

The cage was wheeled into a truck, which pulled away from the loading dock. "Once the dinosaurs are taken away," Owen said, "there's no way to track them."

"We need to save them," Maisie said.

They went back to the grate where they could see the auction below. Eversoll was saying, "And now, a special treat for the truly discriminating buyer! We'd like to preview a new asset we have been developing. We call it . . . the Indoraptor."

An elevator rose from the level of the containment cells up to the garage. In it, the Indoraptor paced in his cage. Once the cage reached the garage level, it was rolled past the steel door onto the cement platform, lit from behind. The bidders saw the silhouette of the powerful Indoraptor and gasped.

"The perfect weapon for the modern age," Eversoll continued. "Built for combat. Tactical response more acute than any human soldier."

The cage rolled forward into the light. When the buyers could fully see the Indoraptor, they whispered to each other, excited. Inside the cage, the Indoraptor paced back and forth like a tiger, making aggressive eye contact with the men in the audience.

Above, Owen, Claire, and Maisie watched through the grate, stunned. "What is that thing?" Claire asked.

"They made it," Maisie said. "Mr. Mills and the other man."

"What other man?" Claire asked.

Maisie pointed down. Claire followed her finger and spotted her former employee, Dr. Henry Wu, glaring at the proceedings.

The Indoraptor hissed. The crowd murmured excitedly. Eversoll raised his hands for quiet. "Designed by Mr. Henry Wu—"

Wu cleared his throat pointedly.

"Excuse me, *Dr.* Henry Wu," Eversoll corrected himself, "the Indoraptor has an intelligence quotient comparable to the *Velociraptor*. Bio specs include echolocation and a heightened sense of smell."

Eversoll nodded to a guard with a rifle, signaling him.

"The Indoraptor has been trained to respond to a pulse-coded laser targeting system," Eversoll continued, "allowing it to isolate and track prey in complex environments."

The guard raised his rifle and flipped on its targeting laser. He focused the beam of light on Anton, the Russian mobster. In the cage, the Indoraptor responded immediately, coiling and focusing intently on the Russian.

Anton looked at Eversoll with confusion and concern.

Suddenly, the Indoraptor leapt toward Anton. Luckily for the Russian, the cage held. The predator snapped at the bars viciously.

"Modifications are still being made," Eversoll said, "but—"

"TWENTY MILLION!" Anton shouted.

Eversoll sucked in his breath, amazed at the bid.

He glanced at Mills, as if to say, *Do I proceed?*

Mills nodded.

The guard clicked off the laser, and the Indoraptor calmed down.

"Do I hear twenty-one?" Eversoll asked.

"Twenty-two!" shouted another bidder.

Watching from above, Owen felt disgusted. He had to do something. "I'll be right back," he said. "Stay here."

"What are you going to do?" Claire asked.

"How should I know?" he admitted.

He put Maisie's hand in Claire's. Seeing that the girl was frightened, he promised, "We're not going to let anything happen to you, okay?"

Maisie nodded. Owen crept out into the hall. Over his shoulder, he said, "She probably shouldn't watch this." Maisie nodded again and put her hands over Claire's eyes.

Down in the garage, the bidding was heating up. The Indoraptor stared daggers at the excited buyers. Anton hungrily bid twenty-five million.

Mills was keeping track of bids on a laptop. Wu went up to him, angry. "What are you doing?" he demanded. "This animal is not for sale!"

"If you want to create an addict," Mills said calmly, "give them a taste."

"It isn't finished!" Wu objected. "It's a prototype!"

"This *prototype* is worth twenty-five million dollars," Mills pointed out. "Right now." Wu still looked furious. "Relax, Henry. We'll make more."

"So will *they*," Wu countered, jerking his head toward the excited bidders. Mills looked at them. Many seemed like pretty shady characters. Still, all that money . . .

Mills gave Wu a look that said his objection was overruled. Wu stormed out.

The bidding for the Indoraptor had reached thirty-two million dollars and was still rising.

In a basement corridor, Owen searched for some way to disrupt the auction. He spotted a fuse box and opened it, unsure of what to do.

DING! Down the hall, an elevator door opened, but the elevator was empty.

Then Owen heard a familiar bray behind him. At the end of the corridor he saw the *Stygimoloch*. She crashed into a steam pipe, seeming disoriented and somewhat frustrated by the unfamiliar experience of being inside a mansion.

Owen looked at the *Stygimoloch,* and then at the open elevator. Idea!

"Hey, buddy," he said to Stiggy. "You're angry, huh? How about we get some of that out of your system?"

CHAPTER
16

This change was inevitable from the moment the
first dinosaur was brought back from extinction.
—Dr. Ian Malcolm

"**T**hirty-seven million!" Anton shouted.

ROOOAARR! The Indoraptor roared and lunged,
testing his cage's bars.

DING! The elevator arrived. A guard stood in front
of the doors, ready for whoever stepped out.

Actually, he wasn't ready.

WHAM! Stiggy ran out of the elevator and head-
butted the guard, who flew fifteen feet and slid to a
stop, unconscious.

The frantic buyers scattered as Stiggy smashed through them like bowling pins. Owen jumped down from the top of the elevator and saw a guard about to shoot her. He sprinted over and slammed his elbow into the guard's face.

The garage was a scene of chaos as buyers and chairs flew through the air, bashed by Stiggy. From his cage, the Indoraptor watched, huffing. He was hungry.

Mills watched as his dream turned into a disaster, and then he slipped out of the room. Eversoll ducked behind the concrete platform.

Owen saw a guard pull a lever, activating the mechanism to roll the Indoraptor's cage out. He knew he had to stop that cage before some buyer made off with the genetic monster. Fighting his way past guards and buyers, Owen pulled the lever hard and broke it. The Indoraptor wasn't leaving.

As Stiggy rampaged around the garage, Owen looked up at the grate, signaling to Claire and Maisie that he'd be right there. They understood.

He raced out of the room, dodging chairs and bodies.

Outside, by the loading dock, buyers scrambled to escape with their dinosaurs, driving off in trucks.

Stiggy crashed out and raced into the forest, free.

"Get this cargo outta here!" Wheatley barked. "Move!"

In the garage, the Indoraptor roared. Wheatley saw an opportunity and headed inside.

Holding a tranquilizer rifle, Wheatley strode toward the Indoraptor's cage. The hybrid dinosaur looked at him, growled, and bashed his head against the bars, rattling the cage. *THUNK!* Wheatley fired a dart into the Indoraptor's neck. He bashed the bars again, furious.

After reloading, Wheatley shot another dart into the Indoraptor. *THUNK!* The Indoraptor dropped to the floor of his cage. Wheatley opened his vest and pulled out a pair of pliers. He looked at the Indoraptor and swapped the pliers for a bigger pair.

He slowly stretched his arm through the bars of the cage, trying to reach the Indoraptor's mouth. But it was just beyond his grasp. If he wanted another trophy tooth, he'd have to go in there.

Wheatley unlocked the door and silently entered the cage. He crouched down and lifted the animal's lip. "Hey, sweetheart," he said, smiling sadistically. "Hope this doesn't hurt too much."

He fitted the pliers around a tooth. But before he could yank it out—the Indoraptor's eye opened. His tail twitched, and his lip curled cruelly.

CHOMP! The Indoraptor clamped his powerful jaws on Wheatley's arm. Wheatley screamed as the hybrid terror rose to his feet, lifting Wheatley off the floor of the cage. A loud snap echoed around the room and Wheatley fell to the ground, one arm now missing. He tried to back away from the Indoraptor. But there was no escape. Only another—

CHOMP!

Hearing Wheatley howl in pain before he died, Eversoll winced. He started to creep from his hiding place behind the concrete platform to the open elevator, trying to be silent.

He made it. When he stepped into the elevator, he found three cowering buyers. He gave them a contemptuous look and pressed the close door button.

DING!

It was the bell from the elevator! The Indoraptor whipped around and raced toward it. Eversoll watched in horror as the doors slowly closed . . . just in time. He exhaled, safe.

Outside the elevator, the Indoraptor turned away in search of other prey. But his tail smacked against the button. The doors opened again. Eversoll stared at the Indoraptor, horrified. The predator leapt into the elevator, making quick work of the four men inside. Their screams reached up to the service tunnel above the garage . . .

. . . where Owen had rejoined Claire and Maisie. Claire covered the girl's ears. Owen knelt down. "Okay," he said soothingly. "Look at me. Stay close to me, okay? I'm gonna go first."

He headed down the narrow tunnel. Maisie took Claire's hand as they followed him. They reached a cross tunnel and saw a door just ahead of them to the right. Owen reached to open it, but then—

"Hold it right there!" a guard barked, advancing on them with his gun aimed. "Drop your weapon to the ground, now!"

Owen slowly took the rifle from his shoulder and placed it on the floor.

"Slide it over," the guard ordered.

He slid it across the floor toward the guard and started to raise his hands. The guard spoke into his radio. "I've got three—"

WHAM! From a cross tunnel, the Indoraptor slammed into the guard like a freight train! Both disappeared into the tunnel. Maisie screamed!

CHAPTER 17

We don't conceive of sudden radical, irrational
change as woven into the very fabric of existence.
Yet I can assure you, it most assuredly is.
And it's happening right now.
—Dr. Ian Malcolm

Owen opened a door behind them. "Come on!"

The Indoraptor came roaring around the corner. Owen slammed the door, but the Indoraptor crashed against it, snapping its jaws. Pushing together, Owen and Claire managed to close the door and turn the lock.

"This way," Maisie said.

In the sub-basement lab, Dr. Wu oversaw the packing of embryos and the Indominus bone, telling a technician to be careful. He grabbed another employee. "You—I need blood samples from the Raptor."

The other employee was actually Franklin!

"Don't stand there like an idiot," Wu snapped. He pointed to a cabinet. "Get me a blood kit." As Franklin rummaged in the cabinet, Wu went to Blue's cage. Zia was nearby with her wrist handcuffed to a pipe.

"I need that animal's blood," Wu said to her.

Blue hissed at him with her claws out.

"Sure," Zia said. "Go ahead."

Wu reached toward Blue, but she snapped, nearly taking his hand off.

"Oh, by the way," Zia added, "her blood is contaminated now."

Putting on rubber gloves, Wu said, "I designed this animal myself. It's pure." He barked over his shoulder, "Kit, please!"

"Yeah," Zia said, nodding, "but I gave her a blood transfusion from a *T. rex*. Not so pure anymore."

Wu's eyes opened wide with anger . . . then surprise as a needle plunged into his neck. Tranquilizers meant for dinosaurs coursed through his system. He groaned as he collapsed, falling through a tray of blood samples.

Standing over him was Franklin, who now looked different—brave, almost heroic.

Zia stared. "Who *are* you?"

"Same guy, different day!" Franklin said, grabbing Wu's keys and unlocking Zia's cuffs.

"Hey!" shouted a big guard. "Step away from the animal!"

As the guard moved toward them holding his gun, Zia reached behind her back and unbolted Blue's cage door. Franklin saw what she was doing.

"I said get away from the cage! Now!"

Zia swung the door open. She and Franklin hid behind it for protection. Blue burst from the cage, killing the guard before he could get a shot off. More guards ran in and raised their guns, and Blue quickly dispatched them, but not before one of the guards fired a shot.

The guard's stray bullet hit a nitrogen tank. *BOOM!* Gas filled the lab as Blue, Zia, and Franklin ran out. An alarm sounded. Lit displays warned: SYSTEM FAILURE.

Owen, Claire, and Maisie entered the darkened library,

knowing Wheatley's men and the Indoraptor were still in the mansion. Maisie pointed to a door at the other end of the large chamber.

They were halfway across when Owen held up his hand. They stopped. He'd seen a dying guard on the floor next to the *Triceratops* skeleton. His laser rifle was next to him. Suddenly, the guard was dragged behind the base of the statue.

The Indoraptor emerged. Done eating the guard, he now stalked Owen, Claire, and Maisie. They crawled around the base of the skeleton. Owen reached for the gun, but the dead guard's radio crackled, catching the Indoraptor's attention.

They looked up. The Indoraptor had climbed onto the *Triceratops* skeleton, claws gripping its horns.

He saw them again.

They ran. The Indoraptor launched after them! They climbed the spiral staircase that led to the mezzanine. The Indoraptor slammed into the bars encircling the staircase, trying to get at them. They scrambled up to the mezzanine. "This way!" Maisie cried.

She led them to a paneled wall in the corner, just as the Indoraptor climbed over the rail from below.

Maisie pulled at the paneling, revealing a hidden door. Owen pushed Maisie and Claire through first before slipping in himself. Claire and Maisie hurried down a ladder into the dinosaur dioramas back on the first level.

Owen opened the door a tiny crack to see if the Indoraptor had followed them. Silence. Then . . . *WHAM!* The predator slammed himself against the door. Owen quickly climbed down the ladder with his heart racing.

Inside the row of dioramas, Owen found a set of switches and shut off the lights. It was dark and silent. They had no idea where the Indoraptor was.

"There's a door at the other end," Maisie whispered.

They made their way through the displays of dinosaurs. In the basement control room, the system rebooted itself, enabling backup power. Lights flickered on.

When Owen, Claire, and Maisie reached the door at the far end of the museum space, it was jammed. As Owen worked on opening it, the lights in the museum space turned on, one by one, until the space was fully illuminated.

Maisie peered at the glass, but because it was

bright inside the diorama and dark outside, she could only see her own reflection. Then lightning flashed outside, and the Indoraptor's face was lit up. He was right on the other side of the glass!

Maisie screamed as the Indoraptor smashed into the diorama!

CHAPTER 18

Our home has, in fundamental ways,
been polluted by avarice.
—Dr. Ian Malcolm

Inside the small space, the Indoraptor thrashed to get at the humans, knocking a huge log into Claire and Owen, trapping them against the wall. "Get away from here!" Claire yelled to Maisie. "Run!"

Maisie ran past the Indoraptor, who slashed at Owen and Claire, wounding Claire in the leg. Claire screamed!

The beast tore free of the diorama. More debris

fell on Owen and Claire, trapping them further. The Indoraptor ran after Maisie, his sharp talons clicking on the library floor.

Maisie sprinted into the foyer, up the stairs, and down the hallway, making for the dumbwaiter. The Indoraptor was close behind her. She dove into the dumbwaiter and slammed the door right in the predator's face.

From inside the dumbwaiter, Maisie was able to ride up to the next floor. But the Indoraptor followed her scent through the wall, raising his head as she rose inside the dumbwaiter. The beast was no longer chasing . . .

. . . it was hunting.

Back in the diorama, Owen and Claire had managed to tear themselves free from the log. But Claire injured her leg in the process and struggled to stand. "Find her," she said.

"I'm not leaving you," Owen said.

"I'm fine. Go!"

Up in her bedroom, Maisie dove under the covers and hid.

Following her scent, the Indoraptor found his way into the dark bedroom. Maisie tried not to breathe as the predator moved slowly across the room, drawing closer and closer. When the terrible creature was just inches away, Owen flung open the door, armed with the dead guard's rifle. The Indoraptor spun to face him.

"Maisie, get down!" he shouted.

BLAM! BLAM! BLAM! Owen fired at the Indoraptor and seemed to wound him. But Owen soon ran out of bullets. The beast rose to his full and terrible height and backed Owen into a corner—

Suddenly, Blue appeared in the doorway! Seeing Owen in danger, Blue attacked the Indoraptor, digging her claws in deep. The two dinosaurs thrashed around the bedroom, destroying it. Pillow feathers hung in the air like snow. Owen dashed across the room, picked up Maisie, and went out the window, climbing to a balcony.

"This way!" Maisie said.

They cautiously made their way around the glass roof over the library.

CRASH! The Indoraptor smashed through a window onto the roof in hot pursuit! Through that same window, Owen could see Blue inside the bedroom, wounded but alive.

To escape the Indoraptor, Owen and Maisie had to climb across the glass roof, and ended up hanging off the side of the mansion from a weather vane. The creature stalked them across the roof, beams straining under his weight. He had almost reached them when—

BANG! BANG! BANG!

They saw Claire behind the monstrous dinosaur, banging on roof beams with the rifle Owen had dropped back in Maisie's bedroom. While the Indoraptor looked at Claire, Owen raised Maisie to a safer spot.

Then Claire turned on the rifle's laser and aimed it . . . at Owen's chest!

The Indoraptor coiled, ready to attack. Owen looked at Claire, realized what she was doing, and winked at her.

With the laser dots still on his chest, Owen ran right toward the Indoraptor. The trained killing machine leapt at Owen, roaring. But at the last second, Owen jumped aside and slid down the roof. The Indoraptor narrowly missed clawing Owen. He landed right on the fragile glass section of the roof and crashed through!

The Indoraptor managed to hang on to a window strut. He began to pull himself back up onto the roof, where he would easily be able to attack Owen and Maisie, but then, from atop the nearby chimney, Blue flung herself onto the Indoraptor's back with a loud screech, causing the awful predator to lose his grip, and both of them plummeted into the library. In midair, Blue reacted quickly and moved to turn the Indoraptor over just in time for—

WHUMP! The Indoraptor landed right on the *Triceratops* skull, impaled on its horns.

Moments later, the elevator doors opened and Zia and Franklin ran into the library. They were stunned to see the dead Indoraptor . . . and also Blue running down another hallway out of the room.

Franklin stared up through the broken skylight and saw Owen, Claire, and Maisie looking down at him. "You good?" he asked.

"Nah," Owen admitted. "You?"

Franklin shook his head. "Nope."

Zia called up to them, "We've got a problem downstairs. You need to see this."

CHAPTER 19

Eighty years ago, nobody could have predicted nuclear proliferation. But then, there it was. And now we've got genetic power. So—how long is it going to take for that to spread around the globe?
—Dr. Ian Malcolm

Mills opened the door to the lab and was shocked to see smoke and flames. He could smell gas. He started to leave, but spotted something on the ground: the glass case holding the Indominus bone. With its DNA, maybe he could start over. He covered his mouth with his handkerchief, darted to the case, and carried it out of the lab.

At the same time, Claire, Owen, Maisie, Zia, and Franklin entered the glass-walled control room perched above the dinosaur cells. Computer screens flashed: VENTILATION SYSTEM FAILURE!

Below them, in the containment cells, small fires burned. A cloud of hydrogen cyanide gas from the lab explosion hung near the ceiling. The dinosaurs ducked their heads down to the floor to avoid the deadly gas.

On another screen, an alert flashed: CONTAMINATION ALERT—HYDROGEN CYANIDE DETECTED!

Through the glass, they watched in horror as the dinosaurs choked on the growing cloud of poisonous gas. "They're dying!" Claire cried.

Owen picked Maisie up and held her. He turned her away from the awful sight of the dying dinosaurs. Claire studied a control board, swiping through a touch screen. She found the command she was looking for. "We can open the cell doors from here."

"Wait, Claire—" Owen said.

She hit the command. The bars on the individual cell doors rose. Dinosaurs hurried out of their cells, gathering in the center of the cavernous chamber. But there was nowhere to go. As the gas moved toward them, they crowded against the main door to the outside.

Claire put her hand over a large red button labeled OPEN OUTER DOORS. She hesitated, torn.

"You push that button," Owen warned, "there's no turning back."

"We can't let them die," Claire said.

"Think about what you're doing," Owen said.

Claire struggled with her decision. To release the dinosaurs into the world was a reckless, dangerous act—probably criminal. But to just stand there and watch them die in agony, roaring and coughing, seemed inhuman.

"Is this who we are?" Claire asked.

"It is today," Owen answered, backing his and Claire's hands away from the button that would release all the dinosaurs into the world. They both exhaled slowly. But then—

BRAAAAANK! BRAAAAANK! BRAAAAANK!

An alarm sounded! A red light flashed! The massive doors swung open and the dinosaurs looked out into the open air.

Owen and Claire spun to see Maisie with her small hand on the big red button. She had tears in her eyes. "I had to. They're alive. Like us."

Below, the dinosaurs scrambled out through the

doors and into the world. They were free.

Near the loading dock, Mills headed toward a van, still carrying the Indominus bone in its glass case. Two guards followed him. Mills heard a rumbling sound and turned around. A *Pteranodon* swept down out of the night sky, picked up one of the guards, and dropped him on the van. *SMASH!*

Now Mills saw where the rumbling was coming from: a horde of dinosaurs was thundering straight toward him. The other guard was crushed in the stampede. Mills dove under the van, avoiding the pounding feet and swinging horns of the animals.

WHAM! Dinosaurs sideswiped the van, sending it sliding. Mills was exposed. He desperately crawled under the van again, leaving the glass case behind, and barely avoiding a stomping dinosaur foot. *WHOMP!*

The van was rocked and hit, and though two of its tires blew, Mills somehow managed to stay safe underneath. The stampede passed. Everything was quiet. Mills breathed a huge sigh of relief.

Then he spotted something a few yards away: the Indominus bone in its glass case. It hadn't been smashed. And it was still worth a fortune. . . .

Smiling greedily, Mills looked around to make

sure it was safe and then crawled out from under the van. He walked over, picked up the case, and grinned.

CHOMP! Out of nowhere, the *T. rex* appeared and bit Mills clean in two! Her massive foot smashed the glass case and the Indominus bone into a thousand pieces. Then she turned and stomped off into the night with a triumphant roar.

CHAPTER 20

Humans and dinosaurs are now going to be
forced to coexist. We will have to adjust to new threats we
can't imagine. These creatures were
here before us, and if we're not careful, they'll
be here after. We've entered a new era.
Welcome to Jurassic World.

—Dr. Ian Malcolm

Owen, Claire, Franklin, Zia, and Maisie left the mansion through the front door and headed down the steps of the entryway. Owen carried Maisie, wrapped in a blanket, in his arms. Claire limped, wounded but glad to be alive.

Maisie's eyes went wide. She gasped, afraid. Blue stood right in front of them.

"Shh," Owen said. "It's okay."

He carefully set Maisie down on her feet. Claire put a reassuring hand on her shoulder.

"She won't hurt us," Owen reassured Maisie. "She's not like the others." He looked Blue in the eye. "Right, girl?"

He spotted an empty cage truck. He slowly moved toward Blue. "See? She's smart. She knows she can't stay here." He beckoned Blue toward the truck as Claire, Maisie, Franklin, and Zia backed away.

"Blue," Owen said firmly, "I need you to come with me. We're gonna go someplace safe."

Blue looked over Owen's shoulder at the cage truck. She'd seen one of those before.

"Blue?" Owen said. "Come with me."

Blue looked at Owen. Then she looked at the line of trees behind her. Freedom. She gave Owen one last look.

Then the sleek predator darted off into the woods toward an uncertain future.

As they watched her go, they realized everything had changed. They now lived on a planet where dinosaurs roamed freely. They could be anywhere— in the forests, in the oceans, and even in the towns.

The group huddled closer together at this thought, and watched as the sun rose on a new world. . . .